MURDER

at WHITEGATES MANOR

ELEANOR TYLER

Chapter One

Miss Catherine Morton was enjoying herself. The party was a gathering of old family friends, and the summer evening was pleasantly warm without being stifling. The room was large and airy, the refreshments were good and the gentlemen were agreeable. If not for the efforts of her hostess to find her a husband, her evening would be perfect.

'I owe it to your dear departed Mama to see you settled,' Lady Walmerstone said. 'I've arranged for you to sit next to Lord Hendley when the musicians arrive, and if he doesn't suit, you must come to my ball next week. There will be plenty more gentlemen there.'

'I won't be here next week,' said Catherine. 'The Carltons have invited me to Whitegates Manor.'

'Whitegates Manor?' Lady Walmerstone looked startled. 'But my dear, isn't that where . . . ?' She broke off suddenly and looked uncomfortable. Then she said, 'Of course, it was all a long time ago. I'm sure you'll have a wonderful time.' Then she excused herself, saying, 'I see my harpist arriving, and I must tell her where to set up her instrument. Now, don't forget, Lord Hendley is very rich and he would make you an excellent husband. Gentlemen are more inclined to like ladies who nod and smile a lot, so make sure you agree with everything he says.'

Catherine thanked her for her advice, then ignored it completely as she settled down for the concert.

It was in the early hours of the next morning that Catherine returned to the London town house, which had been left to her by her father in the absence of a male heir. Her maid, Sally, was waiting for her.

'You talked to Lord Hendley, then?' asked Sally as she helped Catherine to undress and then brushed her long, dark hair. Sally had been with Catherine for so long that she was as much of a companion to Catherine as a maid.

'For an entire half-hour,' remarked Catherine teasingly.

'You should land him, miss, if you want my advice. Land him whilst you can.'

'Lord Hendley is not a fish! Although he does tend to open and close his mouth rather a lot when he can't think of anything to say,' she added.

'And when will you stop making fun of young gentlemen?' asked Sally. 'It's just that kind of nonsense that's landed you up on the shelf.'

'I can't help making fun of them if they are ridiculous. Besides, I see nothing wrong with being on the shelf.'

'You've been reading too much Miss Austen,' remarked Sally, as she tugged at her mistress's hair.

'*A single woman of good fortune is always respectable, and may be as sensible and pleasant as anybody else*,' quoted Catherine. 'And of course Miss Austen is right. I will go even further. A single woman of good fortune is a good deal happier than many married ladies. She may do whatever she wants to do, and may come and go as she pleases. Yes, there is a good deal to be said for being single.'

'There's no talking to you when you're like this,' said Sally with a harumph. 'Let's just hope there's some nice young gentleman at Whitegates who's looking for an awkward wife!'

Catherine laughed. But behind her laughter was something thoughtful, as the name of Whitegates set her to wondering again about what she had heard at the soirée.

'Tell me, Sally, have you heard anything about it? Whitegates, I mean? Although my mother was a friend of the Carltons, I have never been.'

'No, miss. Should I have done?'

'I'm not sure.' Catherine was pensive. 'It's just that Lady Walmerstone behaved rather oddly when I mentioned it this evening. She hinted at the fact that something had happened there.'

'What kind of thing?'

'I don't know. She wouldn't tell me. But it sounded like something bad.'

Sally snorted. 'One of the gentlemen took too much to drink and insulted Lord Carlton, most likely,' she said, unimpressed.

'I expect you're right.'

'There, now you're done,' said Sally, as she bound up Catherine's hair for the night.

Catherine climbed into bed and as her redoubtable maid left her, she blew out the candle.

'So this is Whitegates,' thought Catherine as the

3

carriage turned off the road a week later and rattled through an impressive pair of gates. The gates took their name from the balls of white marble that decorated the top of each pillar, and the house took its name from the gates.

It was an imposing Georgian residence. Large windows flanked the front door in perfect symmetry, gleaming in the summer sun. Gravel walkways surrounded it and meandered invitingly through formal gardens and over immaculate lawns.

The carriage swept around the turning circle and rattled to a halt. The door was opened, the step let down, and Catherine emerged, blinking a little in the bright summer sunshine.

'Miss Morton! How delightful to see you!' said Lord Carlton, coming down the impressive stone steps to greet her.

Lord Carlton was a jovial man of about fifty years of age, dressed in a black tailcoat, cream breeches and buckskin boots. His white shirt was frilled at the wrists and around his neck he wore a cravat.

He made her a bow and kissed her hand, then led her up the steps to the house. The hall was light and spacious. There were gilded chairs and marble-topped console tables standing against the walls. A staircase led upwards from the far end, and it was lined with family portraits.

Having glanced around her, Catherine began to unfasten the strings of her bonnet, just as Lady Carlton came into the hall.

'Catherine! My dear!' she said, coming forward and kissing Catherine on the cheek. 'I have only just been informed of your arrival. You had a good journey, I hope?'

'Very good, thank you.'

They embarked on the customary exchanges, with Lord Carlton enquiring after the horses, and Lady Carlton anxious to know that the sheets in the inns had been aired. Then Lady Carlton took Catherine by the arm and said, 'Come, let me show you to your room.'

Leaving her husband to see to the other guests, Lady Carlton led Catherine up the imposing staircase, chattering all the time. She was a small, birdlike woman, quick and light in her movements. Her manner was superficially easy, but Catherine was surprised to detect a note of unease in her voice.

'Is anything wrong?' she asked, when Lady Carlton at last paused for breath.

There was the merest hint of a pause, and then Lady Carlton said, 'No, of course not. What could possibly be wrong? But here we are. This is your room. I hope you will like it.' She led the way into a beautiful bedroom.

Large windows gave into the gardens, and light flooded the room. A four-poster bed was set against the left-hand wall. In one corner was a writing-table, and next to it was a door leading to a dressing-room.

As Catherine took in her surroundings, Lady Carlton moved around the room with her quick, light movements, now smoothing the red damask counterpane, now adjusting a pair of Sèvres vases that stood on the mantelpiece, one on either side of an ormolu clock.

'It is such a pleasure having you here,' said Lady Carlton. She looked as though she was about to say something, but then changed her mind. 'I'm sure you must be tired after your journey. I will leave you to rest.'

She gave Catherine an affectionate kiss and left the room.

Now what has unsettled her? wondered Catherine. *Has she been having trouble with the servants again? I will no doubt hear all about it soon enough.*

The door opened again and Sally entered the room.

'Would you believe it?' said Sally. 'The footmen had muddled up your boxes. I found them taking your ball gowns to the stables and your saddle to the bedroom! Great lummoxes they are, if I don't have my eyes on them every minute, there's no telling what they'll get up to.'

She was followed by two footmen, who deposited a large box and several bags on the floor by the bed.

'Will that be all?' asked one of the footmen.

'For now,' said Sally, and they departed.

'I think I'll take a turn around the gardens whilst you unpack,' said Catherine. 'I want to stretch my legs after spending so long in the carriage.'

'Very good, miss,' said Sally. Truth to tell, she would find the whole business of unpacking a lot easier without her mistress in the way.

Catherine picked up her gloves and proceeded to make her way downstairs. She paused at the bottom. The sound of conversation was coming from the drawing-room. She did not at present feel inclined for company, and so she found a side door and went outside onto the terrace.

The grounds were looking beautiful. There were rose gardens to her right and wide lawns to her left. In the distance she could see a lake. She decided to stroll through the rose gardens. The roses were just beginning to come into bloom. A few unfurled flowers dotted the banks of bushes, and buds were swelling on the stems. She breathed in, but it was too early in the year to catch their perfume.

She took the steps leading down from the terrace and followed a path through the rose gardens and into the shrubbery. Tall rhododendrons lined the path, and soon they were mixed in with forest trees. The light beneath their canopy was dim, and as Catherine went further into the woodland the air grew cooler.

The path began to lead downwards. To her right hand side the ground fell away, and soon the downward slope at her right was steep enough to make her glad of the rustic railing that edged the path.

Still, she was beginning to feel uncomfortable. The atmosphere beneath the heavily-leafed trees was oppressive, and she felt a sudden unaccountable urge to look round. Not much further along she saw one of the gardeners working below her and she felt a sense of relief. She decided to stop for a while. Leaning over the railing she watched the bent old man as he worked. After a few minutes he looked up and saw her.

'Aarrr,' he said sagely. He put his hand to the small of his back as he straightened up. 'That's where it 'appened. All smashed to pieces she was. Right where you're standing. That's where it 'appened all right.'

'What happened?' asked Catherine.

'Right there. Right by the railing. That's where she fell and broke 'er neck.'

Chapter Two

Catherine shivered. She didn't know if it was the wind or if it was the ghoulish words of the old man, but she was suddenly cold.

'Who?' she asked, wondering as she did so whether she was right to be humouring the old man. For all she knew, he could be of unsound mind. 'That's where who fell?'

'Killed she was, and 'er neck was broke,' said the old man with relish. 'Aarrrr, 'twas a dreadful thing to 'appen, it was.'

'Where who fell?' asked Catherine again.

He pursed his lips and shook his head. 'Fell from a terrible height.'

Catherine wondered if this was what Lady Walmerstone had been talking about at the evening party?

'Pretty little thing,' he said, shaking his head. 'Golden curls she 'ad. Came up be'ind her, 'e did, and —' He broke off, and his manner suddenly changed.

Catherine heard a crunching sound. There were footsteps coming along the path. She turned round and saw a gentleman walking towards her. He was about thirty years of age and would have been handsome had his mouth not been set in such a stern line. His hair was dark and his eyes were brown. She guessed he was a man who spent most of his time outdoors, for his skin was bronzed. He was well dressed in a coat of blue superfine and cream pantaloons, with highly polished Hessian boots.

'Miss Morton, I would hazard a guess,' he said.

She inclined her head, saying, 'That is so.'

'Lady Carlton asked me to look for you. It is almost time for tea. I am Mr Stanton, at your service.'

He made her a slight bow, then offered her his arm.

She took it, glad to feel the solid warmth of it, and they set off back to the house.

'I shouldn't let anything Odgers says worry you,' he remarked as they walked back through the grounds. 'He's an old man, and old men have their fancies.'

'But there was an accident?' she asked. 'Someone did fall?'

'An accident?' He hesitated, and then said, 'An accident. Yes, of course.'

'And do you know who fell?'

'I was not here at the time, it was a long time ago.' Changing the subject abruptly, he said, 'Will you be staying at Whitegates long?'

'For a month,' said Catherine. 'Lady Carlton is an old friend of my mother's, and has kindly invited me to stay for as long as I choose.'

'It's a beautiful house, I'm sure you will enjoy yourself.'

'Have you been here before?' asked Catherine curiously, as they broke free of the woodland and emerged once more into the sun.

'N . . . no.'

Catherine caught the slight hesitation. That was the

—

9

second time he had hesitated, but he did not look like the sort of man who was usually hesitant.

'The riding is very good hereabouts,' he said, again changing the subject. 'Do you ride, Miss Morton?'

'Somewhat,' she said.

He raised his eyebrows. 'Somewhat?' He smiled. It gave a sudden warmth to his face. 'How does one ride "somewhat"?'

Catherine laughed. 'One rides very carefully, over easy country, and never goes too far!'

He joined in with her laughter. 'A good description.'

'Whereas you ride a great deal?' she asked playfully.

'I do - over hard terrain and the further the better.'

'Have you known Lord and Lady Carlton long?' asked Catherine, as they reached the flight of stone steps leading up to the terrace.

They began to climb them and they paused at the top to admire the view.

'I've known Lord Carlton for many years. I met Lady Carlton for the first time two days ago.'

'Do you know any of the other guests?' she asked.

'I've met Lord Gilstead before. We were both in the army, fighting on the Peninsula. I've also met Mrs Maltravers, her daughters, of course, and young Glover. As for the rest, they are new to me.'

'I shall look forward to making their acquaintance,' said Catherine.

They walked on, rounding a corner of the house, and Mr Stanton said enigmatically, 'You may be able to do that sooner than you had intended. Here is Mrs

Maltravers now.'

Mrs Maltravers was a buxom matron clad in a voluminous cape. She was heading towards them, puffing along beside her three very pretty daughters.

'Ah! Mr Stanton! There you are!' she said, giggling as though she was a young girl herself. 'We were just looking for you, were we not my dears?'

The three girls giggled in unison.

Catherine felt Mr Stanton tense. Nevertheless, he replied politely enough. He gave them a slight bow and then made the necessary introductions.

'Now you promised to show us the water garden,' said Mrs Maltravers girlishly, tapping Mr Stanton with her fan. 'There is just time before tea, and we are not about to let you disappoint us, are we girls?'

A chorus of giggles followed her sally.

But Mr Stanton said, 'Unfortunately, I must ask you to wait a little longer. I am just escorting Miss Morton back to the house.'

'Oh, pray don't worry about me,' said Catherine mischievously. 'I can manage quite well on my own. I would not dream of asking you to disappoint Mrs Maltravers, much less her three splendid girls.'

Mrs Maltravers beamed at her. 'Well, now, if that isn't handsome. But won't you come with us, Miss Morton?'

'Thank you, no. I must see if my maid has finished unpacking my boxes.'

'Quite, quite,' said Mrs Maltravers, not displeased to be able to secure such an eligible gentleman for the sole entertainment of her three - unmarried - daughters. 'Well, then, let us go,' she said.

She beamed up at Mr Stanton who, thus

outmanoeuvred, had no alternative but to offer her his arm.

The last thing Catherine heard as she strolled back across the lawn to the house was the high-pitched giggling of Clarissa, Melissa and Felicity as they claimed his other arm.

'And who was the gentleman I saw you walking with earlier?' asked Sally that evening, as she prepared to help Catherine dress for dinner.

'I don't suppose it will do any good to pretend not to know what you're talking about?' asked Catherine.

Sally said nothing, but her shoulders were very expressive.

'Very well, then. That was Mr Stanton.'

'Mr Stanton?' asked Sally.

'Yes.'

'He looked like a very handsome gentleman. What did you talk about? Anything interesting?'

'Yes. Do you know, Sally, I've found out what happened here. It was an accident. A young lady fell from the path into the woodland below and was killed.'

'Ah.' Sally lay out a pair of long white gloves. 'So that's what it was.'

'Yes. 'Catherine's voice was meditative. 'Even so . . .'

Sally turned to look at her. 'Even so?'

Catherine was thoughtful. 'I'd like to know more about it.'

Sally was surprised. 'Why, Miss Catherine? It's not like you to be morbid.'

Catherine picked up her silver-backed hairbrush.

'Maybe not. Even so, there was something about the story that didn't quite ring true.'

'Who told it to you?'

'One of the gardeners. An old man with a bent back. Odgers, Mr Stanton said he was called. He told me that the young lady was smashed to pieces.'

'The old monster!' exclaimed Sally.

Catherine gave a wry smile. 'Yes, he certainly enjoyed trying to shock me. But then, just as he was in the middle of it, he suddenly clammed up. You see, Mr Stanton arrived.'

'And you think the two are connected?' asked Sally shrewdly.

Catherine paused. 'I'm not sure. But when I asked Mr Stanton more about it he was very evasive.'

Sally looked at her mistress thoughtfully. 'His looks haven't blinded you to his character, then,' she remarked.

Catherine shook her head. 'No. They haven't. And neither has his charm. Although I am not saying anything against his character. I know no harm of him. He may be perfectly respectable.'

'No man who looks like that is respectable,' muttered Sally.

Catherine's mouth twitched. But then her thoughts sobered. 'I asked him a number of questions and he either hesitated before answering, as though thinking what he should say, or gave an answer that wasn't really an answer at all.'

'Well,' said Sally, 'I'll see what I can find out from the other servants. There's always gossip in the servants' hall, and that kind of thing's bound to be talked about.'

'Good, Sally. I would like to know a few more details.'

'Such as?'

'Such as, who was the unfortunate young lady? And why does no one - other than the gardener - seem to want to talk about it?'

'You always did have an enquiring mind,' remarked Sally approvingly. 'I'll see what I can do.'

'Now, Sally, which dress do you think I ought to wear tonight?

'I think you should wear the green silk. It's the only one I've had a chance to iron. The others are still creased from the packing.'

Catherine agreed and Sally helped her to dress. Chemise and drawers went on first, followed by a pair of stockings and light stays. Then the green evening dress, with its high waist and long flowing skirt. Then Catherine slipped her feet into dainty satin slippers before seating herself in front of the mirror so that Sally could dress her hair.

'There,' said Sally, when she had arranged it into a chignon and decorated it with flowers. 'It's done.'

Catherine stood up. Sally fastened a string of pearls round her neck and then she pulled on her long white evening gloves.

'Now, you must find out as much as you can about the accident from the servants, and tell me all about it when I return,' she said.

Sally promised, and Catherine went downstairs.

The drawing-room, when she entered it, was already full of people. Mrs Maltravers she recognised, and her three daughters, and also Mr Stanton. Lord and Lady

Carlton were also there. But the other people Catherine did not know.

Lady Carlton came forward to claim her, and introduced her to all those present. There was Lord Gilstead, a fair man with a scar across one cheek - from fighting in the war against Napoleon which was happily now over, guessed Catherine. Then there was young Mr Glover, a good-natured but rather awkward young man; the Reverend Mr Lucas, who had walked over from the rectory in answer to an invitation to dinner; the three Thomas boys, and Mr Edmund Spence.

The ladies were equally diverse. As well as Mrs Maltravers and her daughters, who were giggling and flirting to their hearts' content, there was Miss Dunstan, a garrulous spinster of some five-and-fifty years of age, who was there with her elderly mother; a vigorous woman in her thirties by the name of Lady Cuthbertson and her fluttery companion, Miss Emmeline Rivers. Lady Cuthbertson's husband arrived just as the introductions were being made. He was a quiet man overshadowed by his wife. He squinted at the world short-sightedly, and wore rather a vacuous expression on his face.

'And who is that?' asked Catherine, as she and Lady Carlton walked across the room.

She nodded towards the corner were there was a young woman sitting alone.

'That is Miss Francesca Simpson.'

'A varied party,' said Catherine.

'And here is Mr Stanton, just in time,' said Lady Carlton as the gong sounded. 'He is going to take you in to dinner.'

Lady Carlton's ruse to throw the two of them together was confounded by Mrs Maltravers, who monopolised Mr Stanton as soon as they were all seated. His attempts to extricate himself from her clutches came to nothing, and at last he was forced to give in to her constant flow of conversation with a good grace.

Catherine, enjoying her meal of clear soup, turbot and roast beef - even in the summer Lord Carlton liked his roast beef - turned her attention to her neighbour, Mr Edward Thomas.

Mr Edward Thomas was a shy young man. Nevertheless, Catherine found him to be an interesting companion. It transpired that they shared a love of poetry, and they spent a happy hour discussing the rival merits of Coleridge and Wordsworth.

As soon as the last person had finished eating Lady Carlton rose to her feet and the ladies copied her example, following her from the room so that the men could indulge in cigars and port.

Once in the drawing-room Mrs Maltravers and her daughters went over to the pianoforte, the younger girls half-heartedly playing a duet in an attempt to while away the time before the gentlemen should return. Lady Carlton devoted her attention to the quiet Miss Simpson, whilst Catherine found herself in conversation with Lady Cuthbertson.

Lady Cuthbertson was a hearty woman. Like many wealthy women she was used to getting her own way. In the space of five minutes she had given Catherine her opinion on the government, the Prince Regent, the price of corn and the delinquencies of the poor, her opinions being seconded by Miss Rivers, who agreed, quietly and fussily, with everything she said.

'Oh, I do so agree with you,' said Miss Rivers, pushing her spectacles back up her nose, as Lady Cuthbertson pronounced Princess Caroline, the Regent's wife, a national disgrace.

'Running round Europe like a lightskirt —'

'Shocking!' tutted Miss Rivers.

'Setting up home in Spain —'

Italy, thought Catherine.

'Making all England a laughing stock —'

'Dear, dear,' said Miss Rivers, shaking her head.

'And what does the Regent do about it?'

'What can he do?' murmured Miss Rivers, with a sad shake of her head.

'He can act like a man!' declared Lady Cuthbertson.

'Quite so,' agreed Miss Rivers, effortlessly changing tack. 'Oh, I do so agree. Quite so.'

Lady Cuthbertson was somewhat mollified. 'So, Miss Morton,' she said. 'What do you think of Princess Charlotte's wedding?'

Catherine glanced at Miss Rivers, who was looking at her anxiously, and wondered what she should say. She had no wish to antagonise Lady Cuthbertson, particularly as she knew that Miss Rivers would bear the brunt of that lady's disapproval, but did not know what would please the forceful lady best. 'I think —' she began. When fortunately she was spared by the arrival of the gentlemen. She gave an inward sigh of relief as Lady Cuthbertson turned her attention to Lord Cuthbertson.

Once free of Lady Cuthbertson's attentions she wandered over to the pianoforte. She was disturbed to find that her eyes kept wanting to drift towards Mr Stanton, who was talking to Lord Gilstead by the door, and made a determined effort to fix her attention on the music. But Melissa and Felicity, who had tired of playing as soon as the gentlemen entered the room, quickly finished their duet and left Catherine alone as they tripped across the room to sit beside the Thomas brothers.

Catherine sat down at the instrument herself and began to softly play. Her fingers were not proficient, producing rather uneven notes, but the tone was sweet. Then, having mastered her errant thoughts, she went over to Lady Carlton, who by this time was sitting alone.

'I'm so grateful to you for talking to Edward over dinner,' said Lady Carlton. 'He is a dear boy, but unfortunately he is very shy. Even with the Maltravers girls he is rather restrained, and they are lively enough to draw anyone out of their shell. You were talking about poetry, I collect?'

'Yes,' Catherine said.

At the mention of poetry several more of the guests joined in the conversation, and the evening ended satisfactorily with a general condemnation of Lord Byron and praise for Cowper instead.

It was only as she was leaving the drawing-room that Catherine found her thoughts returning to the nameless young lady who had met with an accident at Whitegates some time before. Who was she? Catherine wondered. And what more would Sally have found out?

She went into her room to find Sally waiting for her. The bed had been turned back and her night-gown was laid out on the bed.

'Did you have a nice evening, miss?' asked Sally. Usually the embodiment of calmness, she seemed strangely agitated, a fact which did not escape Catherine's notice.

'Yes, thank you. But tell me, Sally. Did you manage to discover anything more about the young lady who met with an accident?'

'Yes, miss,' said Sally, helping Catherine off with her gown and into her wrap. 'Only it wasn't an accident, miss. It was murder.'

Chapter Three

'Murder?'

Catherine was shocked. She sat down in front of the dressing-table far more quickly than she had intended.

'Yes, Miss Catherine. That's what they say it was in the servants' hall. They say it was murder.'

Catherine was temporarily dumbfounded. Murder? But then she began to nod. Yes. That would explain it - the reluctance of Lady Walmerstone to tell her anything about it. An accident they would have discussed. But murder? No.

Catherine met Sally's eye in the mirror. 'But who was murdered? And why?'

Sally began to unpin Catherine's hair. 'A young lady, Miss Sophie Winter. She was staying here as a guest in 1814 —'

'Two years ago,' said Catherine thoughtfully.

'Yes, miss. She was here as part of a house party. She came here with an elderly aunt. A lively young lady, she was, and very popular by all accounts.'

'Go on,' said Catherine.

Sally picked up a silver hairbrush and began to rhythmically brush Catherine's hair. 'Well, she was often out and about in the gardens, miss. Then one day, when it was time to dress for dinner, she was nowhere to be found. Her aunt sent one of the maids to look for her, but the maid couldn't find her anywhere. But her aunt wasn't really worried. In fact she was angry, Gladys the chamber maid says.'

'Angry?' queried Catherine.

'Angry because the young lady'd forgotten her manners and was going to be late for dinner,' Sally explained. 'So then the old lady sent one of the grooms out to look for her but he couldn't find her either, and by that time the old lady was getting worried. And then the news came: Miss Winter had been found at the bottom of a steep slope in the woodland, and her neck was broken. She was dead.'

'That doesn't mean it was murder,' said Catherine in surprise.

'I know, miss. That's what I said to Gladys. "That doesn't make it murder," I said. But there's more.'

She put down the brush and helped Catherine out of her wrap and then out of her stays.

'There was a young gentleman, you see,' Sally continued. 'A very handsome young gentleman, staying here at the time. Lord Amundel his name was. He and Miss Winter spent a lot of time together. It was all properly chaperoned, nothing underhand. He taught her how to pull a bow and shoot an arrow, and he rowed her across the lake - that kind of thing. Anyway, on the evening of the murder, he'd come in very late himself. Almost missed the start of dinner, Gladys said. Questions were asked.'

'You mean, had he been with her that evening?'

'That's it, miss. That's what it looked like, you see, though he denied it. He said he'd been riding but his horse had gone lame. He'd had to walk the animal home and that was why he was late.'

'But I don't see how that can lead to an accusation of murder. Even if he was late, it's a far cry from having killed someone. '

'It was believed he'd had an assignation with Miss Winter, you see. And if so, that made him the last person to see her alive.'

'But did no one check the stables to see if he had indeed gone out riding, and if indeed his horse had gone lame?'

Sally shook her head. 'I don't know. No one seemed to know about that. I suppose they wouldn't have liked to do it. It would've seemed they didn't believe him and after all, he was an earl.'

'And so, we have a dead young woman and an absent young man. But there must have been more to it than that. Was there evidence that she had been pushed?'

Sally shook her head. 'None. But if there *had* been an assignation, as everyone believed, then they would have returned to the house together. Instead of which the young gentleman returned alone.'

'It's suggestive, perhaps, but it doesn't seem enough to prove there was a murder. There doesn't even seem to be any proof that there was an assignation. And even if there was, perhaps the two young people had a quarrel, and Miss Winter ran off and tripped over a tree root, falling down the slope.'

Sally nodded. 'Exactly my feelings, and so I said to Gladys. But, you see, not three weeks after it happened he shot himself.'

Catherine was startled. 'Who? Lord Amundel? He *shot* himself?'

'Yes, miss. At his club. Said to his friends that he couldn't live with the guilt, then walked into an empty room and shot himself. Just like that.'

Catherine was silent. 'Well,' she said, a few minutes later, 'that seems conclusive. Did he say *why* he'd killed Miss Winter?'

'No, miss. At least, not that Gladys knows. Just said he couldn't live with the guilt and ended his own life.'

Catherine's face fell. 'What a terrible tragedy. No wonder no one wants to talk about it.'

'No, miss.' Then, ever practical, Sally asked, 'What time shall I wake you in the morning, miss?'

'Sally, you amaze me.'

'No use crying over spilt milk,' said Sally, practical again. 'It's a tragedy as you say, miss, but it's over now. It was all a long time ago.'

Catherine nodded thoughtfully. '"It was all a long time ago." That phrase keeps recurring. And yet, do you know, Sally, I have the feeling that it wasn't. Or, what I mean is, that yes, it was all a long time ago, but that it wasn't *over* a long time ago. The tragedy lingers. It's in the house still. Lady Carlton won't talk about it. There are people who won't stay at Whitegates because of it.'

'But the servants love talking about it,' interjected Sally.

Catherine nodded. 'Yes. One way or another it lingers. And there's something more. I don't know what it is. I can't put my finger on it. But I feel as though it's in the house still. In some strange way, I don't think it *is* over. Ah, well,' she said more briskly, realising how fanciful she was becoming, 'I am probably just tired. Of course it's over. How could it not be? Miss Winter is dead, and her murderer, too, is in his grave. Now that the mystery is solved I can put it out of my mind.'

But that was easier said than done, and her dreams that night were haunted by the image of Miss Winter falling to her death.

The brightness of morning made such fanciful ideas seem ridiculous. Whitegates Manor was a beautiful house, and Catherine was determined to enjoy her stay. The morning was fine, and Catherine was looking forward to her first full day.

She dressed in a jonquil-striped muslin, then went downstairs to join the other guests.

Arrangements were already under way for taking a picnic out to Primrose Hill, a local beauty spot. The idea had originated with Mrs Maltravers: together with her daughters, that lady needed constant diversion.

'We will make a day of it,' Lady Maltravers was saying. 'Melissa, you are sitting on your fan.' This last came out in an admonishing tone and Melissa, duly chastened, rescued the crushed feather item.

'And what do you think of the idea?' murmured a deep voice in Catherine's ear.

She turned to see Mr Stanton.

'I think it an excellent one,' she said. 'As long as the hill is not too far distant.'

'Of course: after your journey yesterday you will not want to spend too long in a carriage.'

'Why, it is not above five miles away!' declared Mrs Maltravers, determined to have a share in the conversation. 'We will not be in the carriage above half an hour.'

'I shall go on horseback,' declared Miss Maltravers.

'And so will I,' declared Miss Melissa Maltravers boldly.

'Nonsense,' said Mrs Maltravers firmly. 'You will travel in the carriage with me. The gentlemen will not run away, my dears, and once we are at Primrose Hill you may flirt with them to your hearts' content.'

She beamed at the assembled gentlemen, who were looking startled, rather than - as she supposed - delighted, at her lack of decorum. Then hiding behind her fan she whispered to Catherine, 'Never fear, my dear. You may be a bit long in the tooth, but there are plenty of gentlemen for us all.'

Catherine gave a gurgle of laughter. She could not be affronted, though she was sure she ought to be, because Mrs Maltravers was so ridiculous!

'Perhaps you would care to ride?' Mr Stanton asked Catherine, adding, with a humorous glint in his eye. 'That is, if your rheumatism permits?'

Catherine's eyes danced. 'Do you know? I think I might.'

'Well!' declared Mrs Maltravers.

Lady Cuthbertson let out a bark of laughter. 'Routed,' she declared, when Mrs Maltravers and her daughters had retired to dress for the outing.

'Oh, yes,' agreed Miss Rivers. Her rôle as companion was so firmly ingrained that she no longer had to think about it, and would have been able to murmur agreeable nothings standing on her head, should it have been required. 'Quite.'

'D'you know, think I might ride myself,' said

Lady Cuthbertson forcefully. 'The exercise will do me good. You can go in the carriage, Emmeline,' she added as an afterthought.

'Oh, yes,' said Miss Rivers, 'the very thing.'

'How about you?' demanded Lady Cuthbertson, directing the full force of her personality towards Miss Simpson, who was sitting quietly in the corner of the drawing-room, in a fit of abstraction.

'Oh! No. I believe I will go in the carriage. I find Lady Carlton's saddles unforgiving.'

'If you wish to ride another day, you must borrow mine,' said Catherine. 'It is softer than Lady Carlton's saddles, and you may find it suits you better.'

'Thank you,' said Miss Simpson with a smile that suddenly lit her face, and showed her to be a very pretty girl. 'I believe I will. If I had thought of it I would have brought my own saddle. I will, another time.'

The two ladies fell into conversation on the merits of various saddles, and parted well pleased with each other. Catherine, for her part, was glad there was at least one sensible female, besides Lady Carlton, she could talk to, and she had a sneaking suspicion that Miss Simpson felt the same.

The ride to the hill was most enjoyable. The day was fine, but not too hot: ideal outing weather.

Catherine experienced a feeling of pleasure as Mr Stanton fell in beside her, riding an impressive black stallion. The animal was spirited, but he controlled it with ease.

'Have you visited Primrose Hill before?' asked Catherine.

'No. As I believe I told you yesterday, this is my first visit to Whitegates.'

'And I should, of course, have remembered everything you said!' remarked Catherine mischievously, her smile taking any sting out of the words.

He smiled, too. 'That is not a very flattering remark,' he replied with good humour. 'I will have you know that I am an extremely eligible bachelor, with a clear income of ten thousand a year. What greater inducement to remembering everything I say could there be than that?'

'To a young lady in search of a husband, surely none,' smiled Catherine.

'But to a lady of your advanced years . . . ' he said with a quirk of the mouth. 'You must remind me to provide you with a blanket for your knees as soon as we reach Primrose Hill.'

Catherine laughed in reply, enjoying his banter.

They rode on, laughing and talking, and the five miles to the beauty spot - which turned out to be nearer eight - quickly passed.

The area was all that Catherine had hoped it would be. Although it was not the time of year for the primroses that gave the hill its name, the area was picturesque and the views were magnificent.

'Does it match your expectations?' asked Mr Stanton, leaning on his pommel and surveying the area.

'Indeed it does.'

He dismounted in one easy movement and then held out his arms. 'May I help you dismount?'

Catherine felt a moment of breathlessness, before

common sense told her that out in the country, with no mounting blocks, she would need help from someone. Bracing herself for his touch she allowed him to help her slide from her horse. Nevertheless, she was unprepared for the shockwave that rolled through her at the feel of his hands around her waist. They lingered for a moment longer than they ought to have done, and then, to her relief as well as her unaccountable disappointment, he dropped them to his sides.

'Mr Stanton! Mr Stanton! Mr Stanton!' Miss Felicity Maltravers was waving mightily as she came towards him. 'Will you lend me your arm?'

Thus appealed to, Mr Stanton could not, as a gentleman, refuse, and with a shrug of resignation he gave her the requested arm.

'Those girls are completely out of control,' said Lady Carlton, coming up behind Catherine.

Then, her brief ill humour dispersing, Lady Carlton gave her attention to her duties as hostess.

Catherine wandered across the hill. The servants were already active, the grooms seeing to the horses whilst the footmen set up the picnic tables. This picnic was to be conducted in style.

She had not gone far when she encountered Mr Glover, who went suddenly bright red.

Catherine smiled. She had not realised how young he was; even younger then Mr Thomas, with whom she had conversed at dinner. Being with an unknown lady was clearly something of a trial for him.

'Are you enjoying the outing, Mr Glover?' she asked him kindly.

He ran his finger round the inside of his cravat, as

if finding it far too tight. And indeed it was tied in such an intricate set of folds it was a wonder it did not choke him!

'Oh! Yes! Dash it all - that is to say - interesting. Yes. Very interesting.'

He looked at her hopefully, like a puppy, and she smiled. 'It is indeed.'

'Might I - that is to say - take my arm?' he offered.

Catherine accepted his offer, and walked with him over the springy grass, doing her best to set him at ease. A few questions about his tailor, an enquiry as to his clubs, and he began to seem more comfortable.

'Dashed nice people, the Carltons,' he said as they returned to the main area, where the picnic was about to begin.

'Very,' said Catherine, noticing at the same time that Mr Glover's eyes, far from resting on Lord and Lady Carlton, were in fact following Miss Simpson.

'The other guests, too, seem very amiable,' said Catherine.

'Miss Simpson's an angel,' declared Mr Glover. 'And dashed plucky.'

Catherine was surprised. Plucky was not a word she would have used to describe Miss Simpson. But to the eyes of love, she thought . . .

'Coming here after everything that happened,' said Mr Glover, his eyes still following Miss Simpson, who was looking fresh and pretty in a spotted muslin walking dress with a matching bonnet and parasol.

Catherine looked at him enquiringly. 'I don't quite understand,' she said.

He looked at her for a moment in surprise, and then said, 'Oh, of course not. You wouldn't do.

You've never met her before, have you? And you weren't here two years ago. Perhaps I ought not to talk about it.'

'If you feel uncomfortable about mentioning it, perhaps you should not,' said Catherine, who was nevertheless consumed with curiosity. Two years ago? That was when Miss Winter had been murdered. But what did it have to do with Miss Simpson? And why did Mr Glover find her so plucky?

'Well, perhaps I ought to, now I've started. Then you'll see just how plucky she is. There was a murder here, you see, two years ago. Miss Winter. She was murdered by her lover. And that's why it's so brave of Miss Simpson to come here. Because she is Miss Winter's cousin.'

Chapter Four

This murder will not go away, thought Catherine.

She shivered, and looked up at the sky. Clouds had built up, and were moving slowly across the sun.

Was it only that morning she had been dismissing as fanciful the idea of the murder still haunting the Manor? In a way, perhaps, it was. And yet the repercussions of it could still be felt, both in people's attitudes to the Manor, and in those whose lives it had touched.

So Miss Simpson was the dead girl's cousin?

That explained her quiet nature.

Even so, Catherine could not fathom why a young lady of a shy and retiring disposition, accompanied only by an old housekeeper for a chaperon, should choose to visit a scene which must hold such unpleasant associations for her.

'Forgive me, Miss Morton, I shouldn't have mentioned it. Only, you see, I'm not used to this sort of thing. I haven't been much in company really. Not with ladies. I keep forgetting they're not like men. I oughtn't to talk about things like murder, I ought to be talking about bonnets. Charming one you're wearing today. And dashed pretty gloves.'

He looked at her beseechingly, and she gave him a smile in reply. 'You are too kind.'

He relaxed a little.

'I ought to be taking you over to the table,' he said, his brow furrowed in concentration as he tried to remember all he had ever been taught about dealing with young ladies. 'Helping you to something to eat. The Carltons have a marvellous cook. Try the venison pasties. The pastry's as light as anything.'

He guided her self-consciously over to one of the tables, on which the food had been spread, and helped her to a plate of tempting delicacies, then found her a place on one of the picnic rugs so that she could eat her meal.

The food was indeed excellent, and the wine was very good.

Mr Glover's attention again wandered to Miss Simpson.

'I do believe Miss Simpson is in need of some assistance,' said Catherine innocently. 'I wonder if I might prevail upon you to help her?'

Mr Glover beamed. 'Well, if you think so . . . '

A nice young man, thought Catherine, as he left her to attend to Miss Simpson, before tucking into her venison pastie.

Her meal finished, Catherine wiped her fingers daintily and then looked about her. As her eyes drifted over the small clusters of people who were busily eating and drinking she found herself wondering about the other guests. Were any more of them connected with the murder in some way? she wondered. Had any of them been guests at Whitegates two years before when the murder had taken place?

As Sally had said, she had an enquiring mind.

But still, she must not become morbid. Taking a

slight interest in a murder that had happened two years before was perhaps natural, but allowing it to dominate her thoughts was unhealthy and she resolved to turn them in another direction.

In this she was helped shortly by Lord Gilstead.

The nobleman, seeing she was alone, took the liberty of sitting down next to her.

'Miss Morton,' he said. 'I was hoping to have an opportunity to speak to you. I believe you know Mrs Granville, my aunt?'

It was the perfect antidote to her morbid thoughts. Mrs Granville was a good-humoured widow whom Catherine had met in London, and the two of them had gone on a number of excursions together.

'Yes, I do indeed. I did not know you were related.'

'I have not been in London very much recently,' he said. 'First with being in the army, and then because I felt the quiet of the country might better suit my nerves.'

'Ah, yes,' said Catherine quietly. 'The war must have been very terrible.'

'Men killing men is always terrible,' agreed Lord Gilstead. 'But with a tyrant like Napoleon on the loose the war had to be fought.'

'He was - is - an extraordinary man,' said Catherine. 'It is just a pity he could not have put his talents to a different use.'

Lord Gilstead gave the ghost of a smile. 'But then, I believe his talents were for domination, and those talents cannot very well be channelled into other uses. They are best suited to war.'

'It is a pity for us he did not decide to dominate his

family, and limit his war-like nature to ruling his home with an iron hand,' smiled Catherine.

He laughed. 'It would, indeed, have made life easier. Still, the war is over now.'

'There you are, Lord Gilstead.' Mrs Maltravers' voice rang out archly as she bore down on Catherine and Lord Gilstead with Clarissa and Melissa in tow. 'I have just been saying to my girls, "We have not seen anything of Lord Gilstead all day," and here you are with Miss Morton. You must not monopolise him you know, Miss Morton,' she said to Catherine. 'Gentlemen find it forward.'

Lord Gilstead threw Catherine a speaking glance. Catherine smiled into her napkin but did not take issue with Mrs Maltravers, for there would have been no point.

'We are in need of an escort to venture further afield, for I am sure we are none of us brave enough to go alone,' Mrs Maltravers continued.

Lord Gilstead may not care much for Mrs Maltravers, but he knew where his duty lay.

'Then you must allow me to go with you,' he said. 'I would be happy to protect you from whatever dangers may be lurking there.'

Mrs Maltravers beamed, his gentle irony lost on her, and claimed him for her daughters and herself.

'Oh! I do declare it is good to have a few minutes to myself,' said Lady Carlton as she sat down beside Catherine later that afternoon. 'You must forgive me, my dear, if I don't feel I have to entertain you. You seem more like family than a guest.'

Catherine was pleased for Lady Carlton to see her

in this way, and was glad that her hostess felt able to relax with her.

'Still, it all seems to be going very well.'

'Yes.' Catherine looked around her, taking in the different small groups: one strolling down the hill and one sitting and talking amongst themselves. 'It seems a very successful party.'

A shadow passed over Lady Carlton's face.

'What is it?' asked Catherine.

Lady Carlton gave a sigh. 'A successful party? I'm not sure about that. I was talking merely about the picnic.'

'Don't you think the party is successful?' asked Catherine curiously.

Lady Carlton shook her head slowly. 'It worries me.'

Catherine was at a loss. 'What does?'

'Why she wanted to come.'

Catherine was thoughtful. Could it be that Lady Carlton was referring to Miss Simpson?

'When she wrote to me I felt as though it was the least I could do, but now I am beginning to wonder if it was wise.'

'Are we . . . are you talking about Miss Simpson?' asked Catherine.

Lady Carlton nodded. 'Yes.' Her face suddenly changed. 'But I was forgetting. Of course, you don't know anything about it.'

'You're wrong. I know all about the murder.'

Lady Carlton shivered. 'Hateful word. But yes, that is what it was. Murder. To think it should have happened at Whitegates.' She shook her head.

'And now Miss Simpson is here, at the scene of the

murder.'

'It's all wrong. But of course, when she said she could not find some of her cousin's effects and wondered whether they might still be here I did not feel I could refuse her an invitation.'

'After two years?' queried Catherine.

'I know. It does seem odd. But she has been away at school, you see, and has only just discovered that certain items are missing. Or at least, that is what she says.'

'Wouldn't her parents have discovered they were missing at the time?'

'They were too shocked by the tragedy, Miss Simpson says: they simply didn't notice.'

'Couldn't you have looked for them and then sent them on? Or asked the servants to look for them?'

Lady Carlton sighed. 'That is what I suggested - I offered to search Miss Winter's room myself. But Miss Simpson said she would rather not specify what had been lost, and would like my permission to search the other rooms, as well as her cousin's, and in addition she would like to search the grounds. I thought it unhealthy, but still I did not feel I could refuse. And I told her that she must stay for as long as she wanted to.'

'You regret it?' asked Catherine.

'Yes. I feel it was a mistake. I should have invited her for no more than a week. You see, she has simply stayed on for the house party.'

'Was that her intention?' asked Catherine.

'I don't know. It was certainly not mine. Too many memories . . . I have nothing against her, as you can imagine, but I don't want the rest of my guests to be reminded of such an unhappy time.' She looked across at Miss Simpson. 'She does not look happy, poor child.'

'Her parents should not have let her come,' said Catherine decisively. Then asked, 'Has she found what she was looking for?'

'She says not. Not yet.'

'And you have no idea when she intends to leave?'

'None at all. But she will have to leave when the house party is over, as we will be going to Lyme for a few weeks. Still, I mustn't burden you with this, my dear. You are here to enjoy yourself.'

'I am doing,' said Catherine.

'Good. I'm pleased to hear it. What do you think of Mr Stanton?' asked Lady Carlton casually.

Catherine's eyes twinkled. 'This would just be an innocent question?' she asked impishly.

'Of course,' said Lady Carlton with a twinkle of her own.

'I think he is the most attractive man I have ever laid eyes on.'

'Ah!' Lady Carlton's exclamation spoke volumes.

'But I have no intention of falling in love with him,' said Catherine.

'None?' queried Lady Carlton.

Catherine laughed. 'I admit, it would be tempting. But falling in love would involve me in too many difficulties. I would then have to choose between the man I loved and my freedom, and I don't want to have to make such a choice. I don't think I could bear to lose my freedom.'

'Perhaps not. But just think what you would stand to gain.' With these words, Lady Carlton stood up.

'Well, I suppose I must return to my other guests. Fortunately they seem to get on well together. Even Mrs Maltravers cannot dampen the atmosphere. And the gentlemen are taking her impertinences very well.'

'There's no real harm in her,' said Catherine.

Lady Carlton frowned. 'N . . . no,' she said hesitantly.

Leaving Catherine to wonder, as she watched Lady Carlton walking away from her, just exactly what she had meant.

'Have you enjoyed yourself, Catherine?' asked Lord Carlton as the day drew to its close. The servants were packing away the remains of the picnic, and the ladies were climbing into the carriages, tired but happy, and ready to return to the Manor.

'Yes, thank you, I have.'

'Good. There's nothing like a picnic to put some colour in your cheeks. Tell me, if you are not too tired, will you favour me with a game of chess this evening?'

'You know I am hopeless at chess!' said Catherine.

'I ought to contradict you, but truthfulness forbids it,' laughed Lord Carlton. 'Nevertheless, you are the only person who plays here and it is a long time since I have had a game. And I am not such a good player myself.'

'Very well,' said Catherine. She felt pleased that Lord Carlton did not stand on ceremony with her, and did not feel the need to pay her flowery compliments. 'I enjoy an occasional game of chess.'

'Good. Then it is settled.' He looked at her horse, which the groom was just bringing forward. 'Are you sure you want to ride back to the Manor?' he asked her.

'I am a little tired,' she confessed.

'There's plenty of room in the carriages. Why not go back with Lady Carlton and I?'

The matter being conveniently settled, Catherine took her place beside her hostess. The carriage was soon on its way and before long was turning in at the gates of the Manor.

As Catherine went into the house she happened to be behind Miss Simpson, and could not help wondering why Miss Simpson had been so eager to visit the scene of her cousin's death.

And what it was she hoped to find.

Chapter Five

'May I borrow your saddle?'

Catherine was sitting in the library the following morning. The windows were open, letting in the fresh summer air. She looked up from her book to see Miss Simpson standing hesitantly by the doorway.

Miss Simpson was a young lady of some eighteen years of age. Large green eyes gave her an appealing, if sad, look, but knowing something of her history Catherine understood why that should be. She was dressed demurely in a white muslin gown, and her light brown hair was dressed in a fashionable chignon.

'I don't mean to interrupt you, but you did say yesterday that if I cared to try out your saddle . . . '

'Yes, of course,' said Catherine, laying down her book and inviting Miss Simpson to join her.

The young lady hesitated for a minute and then joined her on the window-seat.

'You mean to go for a ride, I take it?' said Catherine, by way of starting a conversation.

'Yes. I like to take some exercise every day, and as there are no excursions planned I thought I would ride out this morning.'

'Have you decided where you mean to go?'

'To begin with I mean to ride down the drive and then turn off towards the lake. After that, I have not decided.'

'I have not yet been out to the lake. How far is it from the house?'

'Not far. About a mile.'

'You seem to know your way around very well,' Catherine remarked.

Miss Simpson flushed slightly. 'I have been here for some time.'

'Ah. You came before the rest of the party arrived, I collect?' she asked.

Miss Simpson nodded. 'Yes.'

'Have you known the Carltons long?' Catherine was curious about the young girl, but her questions were not prompted solely by curiosity. She felt that Miss Simpson was unhappy and might be in need of someone to turn to. She hoped that if the young girl was lonely or confused she would feel she could turn to her.

Miss Simpson flushed again. 'No.'

She was not more forthcoming, but as she started to rise Catherine said, 'I have known Lady Carlton since my childhood. She was a friend of my mother's. Strangely enough, though, I have never visited Whitegates before. Is this your first visit too?'

Miss Simpson nodded.

'It seems to be an impressive house. I have a beautiful room. It overlooks the terrace.'

'Mine is at the back of the house,' said Miss Simpson.

'Oh, I'm sure Lady Carlton would find you a room at the front if —'

'No. Thank you.' Miss Simpson was becoming agitated. 'I asked for that room.'

———

'Ah.' Catherine sounded surprised. 'But I thought you said you had not been here before?'

Miss Simpson looked as though she was about to speak. Then, standing up, she said, 'If you are sure it will not inconvenience you to lend me your saddle?'

'Of course not. I have already spoken to the grooms. I hope you will find it comfortable.'

Some of Miss Simpson's stiffness left her as the topic turned into more neutral channels. 'It can't be any worse than Lady Carlton's saddle. I don't know how she manages to ride for more than ten or fifteen minutes.'

Catherine gave a humorous smile. 'Lady Carlton has not ridden in years!'

Miss Simpson smiled too. 'That explains it. I hope to be back before luncheon; you may wish to ride yourself this afternoon.'

Catherine returned to her task of choosing a book. She was not displeased with the morning's conversation. She felt she had made a start in getting to know Miss Simpson, and for the time being she could do no more. She could not force the young girl to confide in her, but perhaps in time Miss Simpson would do so. For Catherine could not disguise from herself the fact that she was curious about the young lady's quest.

Outside the window the three Thomas boys were instructing the three Misses Maltravers in the use of a bow and arrow. It was obviously a favourite pastime, as comments on the previous day's efforts kept floating through the window. The young couples were well suited, Catherine decided. The three Thomas boys, lively and jolly, and the Misses Maltravers, if a little silly, equally gay.

Yes, she was getting to know her fellow guests. The only one she had not yet spoken to, she realised as he walked past the window, was Mr Edmund Spence.

Having spent the morning watching the archery practice - an occupation that had drawn most of the guests out into the garden - Catherine returned to her room to tidy herself before lunch.

Sally was not there, but Catherine had only to tuck in a few stray strands of hair and smooth the crown with her brush to make herself presentable, and she did not need her maid's help for that. She sat down at her dressing-table. She was just repairing the damage to her hair when the door opened. To her surprise, the mirror showed her Miss Simpson.

'Did you enjoy your morning's ride?' asked Catherine, thinking Miss Simpson must have come to thank her for the loan of the saddle.

'A good question,' said Miss Simpson cryptically as she entered the room, closing the door behind her. 'I would never have guessed it was you,' she said, fumbling for something in her reticule. 'You weren't even here two years ago. But now I know. It's no use pretending,' she went on, seeing Catherine's startled face. 'But there's just one thing I want to know. Why did you do it?'

Catherine could not think what Miss Simpson was talking about. 'I don't know what you mean.'

'No?' Miss Simpson apparently found what she was looking for, and to Catherine's shocked surprise she drew a pistol out of her reticule. 'Perhaps this will sharpen your wits.'

'Have you gone mad?' asked Catherine in astonishment.

'It's not me who's mad. Maybe it's you. Maybe that's why you did it. Maybe you were jealous. Maybe you couldn't bear her to have something you couldn't have. It takes people like that sometimes, I believe, when they get past a certain age. They can't bear anyone else to be happy because they're so unhappy themselves. Is that what it was?'

Catherine looked hesitantly at the pistol. Her instinct was to go over to Miss Simpson and take the gun out of her hands, which were trembling: it was clear the young lady was uncomfortable with the weapon. But because of this trembling Catherine decided not to move. In her present nervous state Miss Simpson might pull the trigger accidentally and that would be a calamity for them both.

'I assure you I don't know what you're talking about,' she said as calmly as she could. 'Won't you tell me what is troubling you? Perhaps together we can put it right.'

'Is that what you said to her? Is that how you put her off her guard?'

'Are you . . . are you talking about your cousin? Miss Winter?' asked Catherine, trying to find her way through Miss Simpson's confusing accusations.

'As if you didn't —'

The door opened and Sally, already apologising for not being there to help Catherine tidy herself for luncheon, walked into the room.

Miss Simpson dropped her hands in front of her, instinctively hiding the gun in the folds of her skirt.

Catherine watched. To her surprise she did not feel

alarmed. Rather, she was curious as to how Miss Simpson would deal with the situation.

'Thank you for the loan of your saddle,' said Miss Simpson, with impressive self-command. 'It was . . . a revelation.'

And then, still with the gun concealed in the folds of her skirt, she backed her way out of the room.

'What was all that about?' asked Sally, sensing that all had not been well.

Catherine shook her head. 'I don't know.' She wondered whether to confide in Sally but then decided against it. Whatever the reason for Miss Simpson's strange behaviour, Catherine felt she would like to get to the bottom of it before speaking of it to anyone else. 'Who will ever understand the young?' she said lightly.

Sally gave a wry smile. 'You're talking like you're a hundred years of age,' she said.

Catherine laughed.

'Now,' said Sally, dismissing the incident, of which she had seen nothing but an unexpected visitor in her mistress's room. 'I think I'd better see to your hair.'

Catherine was distracted through luncheon.

Miss Simpson had not put in an appearance, and Catherine was not surprised. The girl had clearly been very upset, if not to say unbalanced, and a few hours rest in her room - she had learnt from Lady Carlton that Miss Simpson "had a headache and would not be joining them" - was probably just what she needed.

And then, thought Catherine, once she has calmed down, I mean to get to the bottom of her strange

---

appearance in my room and her even stranger accusations.

As she was leaving the dining-room, luncheon being over, she was surprised to feel a hand on her arm. She did not need to look round to know whose hand it was. There was only one man who could make her skin burn with the slightest touch, and that man was Mark Stanton.

'What is it?' he asked her, *sotto voce*, as the other guests proceeded to the drawing-room.

'What is what?' she asked, swallowing: his presence unnerved her in the most disturbing way.

'You're distracted.'

'I'm —' She stopped. No matter how compelling she found him, she did not trust him enough to confide in him. 'It's nothing. A slight headache,' she said.

'There seems to be a spate of them.' He looked at her searchingly as he spoke, and she could tell from his tone that he did not believe her.

'It's the weather,' she said.

As if to lend veracity to her statement, there was an ominous rumble from overhead: it seemed a storm was on its way.

He regarded her searchingly for another minute and then, pretending to accept her excuse, he let go of her arm. Then he followed her from the room.

'Ah! You're here,' said Lady Carlton, trying to hide a smile at the fact that Catherine and Mr Stanton had been a minute or two longer than was strictly necessary in getting from the dining-room to the drawing-room.

Miss Maltravers let out a long sigh. She was looking out of the window at the rain, which had begun to sheet down from the leaden sky. 'What are we going to do?' she asked of no one in particular. 'I can't abide the rain.'

There were a few more sighs from her sisters, and a few shufflings from the Thomas boys, who had promised to take the Maltravers girls for a row on the lake.

Mr Spence gave an ostentatious cough.

Catherine turned to look at him. She had not had an opportunity to get to know him yet, and she now gave him her full attention. He was an affected young man with long hair brushing his collar and a theatrical air. His clothes were flamboyant, and looked to be extremely uncomfortable. The points on his shirt collar were so high that he had difficulty in turning his head, and his coat was so tight it must surely pain him to breathe. His waistcoat was elaborately embroidered, and his breeches did not show a single wrinkle.

'Yes, Mr Spence?' asked Lady Carlton. 'Do you have a suggestion to make?'

'Only that you might care to read through my play.'

He spoke with a carefully studied air of nonchalance, and could not have hoped for a better reaction to his suggestion than the one he received. The Maltravers girls, instantly perceiving the opportunity for fun and frivolity, were in raptures. The afternoon had seemed to stretch out endlessly before them, with the weather keeping everyone indoors, but performing a play would pass the time most agreeably and would furthermore give them an opportunity to be the centre of attention.

'Oh, yes!' said Clarissa.

47

'The very thing,' declared Melissa.

With Felicity adding, 'I love the theatre!'

Their comments were echoed by the Thomas boys, and the older guests declared that, whilst they were not inclined to act themselves, they would find watching a performance most agreeable.

Thus it was decided. The Maltravers girls, together with their mother - who had no intention of being left out of such an enjoyable occupation - and the Thomas boys were to be the actors, and Mr Spence was to direct.

'Though that will leave us short of one gentleman,' said Mr Spence with a frown. He turned to Lord Cuthbertson, an elderly and rather old-womanish gentleman who was peering at him short-sightedly . 'Sir Toby Entwhistle would be just the part for you.'

'Oh, no, no, no,' said Lord Cuthbertson, alarmed. 'Oh, no, that wouldn't do at all.'

'Of course not!' snorted Lady Cuthbertson. 'Far too strenuous. Emmeline, you will take the part.'

'Oh, no, Lady Cuthbertson. The part would be played so much better by you,' declared Miss Rivers.

Catherine hid her smile behind her fan. Miss Rivers was so conditioned to flattery that even in this case she must defer to her employer.

'But Miss Rivers is a woman!' exclaimed Mr Spence, startled.

'Emmeline's a capital actress. She can play anything she turns her mind to,' said Lady Cuthbertson. Her tone brooked no argument.

Catherine looked at Mr Spence with interest. He had to either accept Miss Rivers as an actor, or cast aspersions on her stated prowess. A battle was waged within him, but with a furtive look at Lady Cuthbertson, who was a formidable adversary, and a rifle through his script, which showed Sir Toby's part to be no more than two or three lines, he finally gave in.

The actors departed to the library, and general conversation among the other guests ensued.

The time passed surprisingly quickly. Lord and Lady Carlton were conscientious hosts, and just before afternoon tea was due to be served the actors returned. Tea was duly served, after which, with a great flourish, Mr Spence introduced his play.

'*Peril at the Abbey*, or *The Mad Monk*,' he announced.

Peril at the Abbey turned out to be a convoluted tale of love and betrayal, with a young couple torn cruelly apart by the evil Sir Toby Entwhistle. What with a clever serving maid, a bold footman, a cruel aunt, a ghostly woman and the eponymous mad monk, the play entertained them for the rest of the afternoon. The Misses Maltravers turned out to be surprisingly disciplined actresses, whilst the Thomas boys strode about the room like men possessed. Miss Rivers was nothing short of astonishing. Whether Lady Cuthbertson had known her companion was a gifted actress, or whether she had simply made the claim and by chance been proved right, Catherine did not know, but indeed Miss Rivers made an excellent Sir Toby. Her air and posture, her carriage and voice, all took on a masculine air, and with the right clothes she could, Catherine believed, have passed for a man.

The only weak link was Mrs Maltravers, who came on at all the wrong points and could never remember her lines. However, the play passed off very creditably and Mr Spence was heartily congratulated.

'Nothing . . . a mere trifle,' he said, obviously highly gratified.

'I do declare, I hope it may rain tomorrow,' said Melissa Maltravers, with an arch look at Mr Spence. 'Then we may have another play.'

Catherine was in her room, engaged in the pleasant occupation of deciding which of her evening gowns she should wear. Clothes were her main extravagance, and now that she was past the years of girlhood she had a wider range of colours and fabrics open to her. Young girls generally wore white, although colours were becoming more fashionable of late, but strong colours were still denied them. It was something that had always annoyed Catherine in her youth. A minor annoyance, to be sure, but still it was one she was happy to be rid of.

'The amber crape?' asked Sally, as Catherine took it out and laid it on the bed. 'What jewellery will you wear with it? The garnets?'

'No. I don't think so. I think the pearls.'

Sally nodded. 'They'll look very well. And the pearl combs for your hair?'

Catherine was thoughtful. She had a new head-dress with an amber plume which she was tempted to wear, but she felt it would be too ostentatious. Plumes were all very well at London balls, but she felt that a country house party demanded something a little more restrained. 'Yes. The pearl combs.'

Sally set to work, and half an hour later Catherine was becomingly attired in the amber crape evening dress, its high waist ornamented with satin ribbon, and its sleeves and hem trimmed with a band of embroidery.

She pulled on her long evening gloves and was just about to pick up her fan when a loud scream rent the air. She looked at Sally; Sally looked at her; and then recovering from her momentary shock Catherine ran out of the room. The scream had come from the end of the corridor. Following the sound, which had now given way to hysterical moaning, she almost ran into one of the maids, who was bolting towards her.

'What is it?' asked Catherine, taking hold of the girl.

'Oh, miss, it's that awful . . . ' sobbed the girl.

'Pull yourself together,' said Catherine sharply. She had had experience of dealing with people in the grip of hysterics and had found that the best way to deal with them was to assume an authoritative manner.

'Yes, miss,' mumbled the girl, giving a half curtsey, 'Sorry, miss. But it's that horrible, miss. She's covered in blood. It's something dreadful.'

Deciding that she would find out exactly what had happened more quickly if she went to see for herself, Catherine went towards the room from which the maid had just emerged. Bracing herself for what she might find she went in.

She saw at once what had happened. A young woman was lying on the bed. Next to her, at an odd angle, fallen from its place on the wall, was a painting of a classical scene. The young woman's head was covered in blood.

Taking a deep breath, Catherine went over to the bed. She felt an inclination to become hysterical herself, but a strong need to know whether the young woman was dead or merely injured overcame the urge. She felt for a pulse, but could not find one. She stood back, shaking, looking at poor Miss Simpson, whom she now knew to be dead.

She turned away from the bed feeling suddenly sick. She swayed slightly - to be caught by strong arms. Another minute and she was being cradled to a firm chest. She put her arms unthinkingly around Mr Stanton and wept unashamedly against him.

'Come,' he said, 'you have had a shock.'

She nodded mutely, and allowed him to lead her over to a chair in the corner, where she sat with her head bowed for a minute until she felt more the thing.

'Foolish,' she said, shaking her head. 'Pray, forgive me. I don't know what came over me.'

'An understandable reaction,' he said. 'It's not a pretty sight.'

'Oh, no!'

The ejaculation came from the doorway, and Lady Carlton entered the room.

'Don't look,' said Mr Stanton, going over to Lady Carlton and blocking her path. 'The poor young woman is dead. Nothing you or I or anyone can do now can help her. I suggest you fetch your husband.'

'I'm right here,' said Lord Carlton, who had hurried upstairs as soon as he had heard the commotion. 'Thank you, Stanton. If you would see Miss Morton back to her room I will see to things.'

Mr Stanton nodded, and offered Catherine his arm.

'Come, Miss Morton,' he said. 'There is nothing more you can do.'

She stood up, still a little shakily, and took his arm.

It felt warm and strong and comforting. He fastened his hand over hers and escorted her back along the corridor.

'Not my room,' she said. 'No, please,' she said firmly, stilling his protest. 'I am quite all right now, I do assure you, but I don't want to be alone.'

'Your maid . . . ' he said.

'Yes, Sally will be there, but I feel a need for company. Oh dear,' she said, flushing, as she realised that her words could have an unfortunate meaning, 'I didn't mean —'

'I know exactly what you mean. Have no fear, I am not about to take advantage of you. Perhaps we should go to the library. I think, as things stand, we have a good chance of being undisturbed there.'

She nodded, and they went downstairs.

'Here,' he said, handing her a glass once he had settled her in an armchair.

She noticed that his hand, too, was shaking.

He saw her notice and said, with a wry smile, 'Yes. Men are human too. We are not made of steel as we like to pretend - and as ladies like us to pretend. We are made of flesh and blood like everyone else. This is not the first time I have seen death. I have seen it many times before on the battlefield. But to see a young lady killed - it isn't pleasant.'

She nodded.

'You'll feel better with this inside you,' he said, as he handed her the glass. 'Drink it. It will do you good.'

'What is it?' she asked, looking at the contents. Then, recognising it by its smell, said, 'Brandy. I don't like —'

'Drink it,' he said sternly.

She pulled a face but did as he said. She was still feeling shaky, and knew that he was right: it would do her good. She felt a burning sensation as it slid down her throat and pulled a face.

'You like it?' he asked, smiling gently as he saw her face.

'It's foul.' She coughed and put the glass on the table next to her. 'How you gentlemen can drink it for pleasure I will never know.'

'You haven't finished it,' he told her.

'And I don't intend to.'

'I refuse to talk to you until you do.'

'Is that thought meant to disturb me?' she asked wryly.

'I hope so.'

The atmosphere had suddenly changed. There was a new note in his voice. It seemed deeper, and was possessed of a smouldering quality that set her inside on fire. It was enlivening and exciting. It was also rather frightening.

She began to speak, but her mouth was unexpectedly dry and no sound came out.

'Now,' he said, his voice once more taking on a matter-of-fact tone as he saw how deeply she was affected, 'why don't you finish the brandy. And then you can tell me what Miss Simpson was doing in your room before lunch.'

Chapter Six

'How do you know about that?' Catherine asked in amazement.

'That is what you wanted to talk to me about, isn't it?' he asked.

She regarded him steadily. 'You haven't answered my question.'

He gave a wry smile. 'Miss Morton, has anyone ever told you that intelligence in a woman is a most inconvenient thing?' he teased.

She laughed. 'Often!'

'So, why was Miss Simpson in your room?'

Catherine sighed, and sat back in her chair. The brandy was doing its job. She felt calmer, as though her nerves were no longer jangling and were beginning to relax. 'I don't really know. It was all very strange.' She paused to collect her thoughts, and then gave him a brief account of Miss Simpson's visit to her room.

'What did it all mean?' he asked with a frown.

She shook her head. 'I don't know. But I mean to find out.'

He looked at her shrewdly. 'You don't think it was an accident, do you? Miss Simpson's death.'

She pursed her lips. 'I don't know. It seems too tidy somehow: Miss Simpson has what seems like a deranged outburst, and then she is conveniently put out of the way. But perhaps I am making too much of it. Perhaps it was an accident, after all. I can't really believe someone would try to murder her by cutting through the cord on the picture - and that's if the cord was even cut through. I have only my imagination to suggest that such a thing might have happened.'

'That would be the first thing to check,' acknowledged Mr Stanton.

'You don't think I'm mad,' said Catherine. It was a statement, not a question.

He shook his head. 'No, I don't think you're mad. I think it's possible. After all, it won't be the first murder to take place at Whitegates Manor.'

'You know about the first one?'

'Yes.'

'But you didn't want me to know.' Again it was a statement. Because by his very presence he had silenced the gardener.

He folded his arms across his powerful chest. 'I didn't want you to worry.'

She accepted his answer, but had he given her the real reason? She did not know. However, she had enough to think about for now.

'I don't think I can return to Miss Simpson's room,' she said. 'But we do need to know whether the picture cord had been cut through.'

'I'll go back. I should be seeing if Lord Carlton needs assistance in any case.'

'Thank you.'

He made her a slight bow.

'And will you check the stables?' he asked. 'If Miss Simpson went out riding this morning she may well have taken a groom. If so, he can tell us if she met someone or saw something on her ride that might have given rise to her outburst.'

Catherine nodded. 'Yes.' She stood up.

'Are you up to it?' he asked.

There was a note of genuine concern in his voice which made her feel strangely vulnerable. 'Yes,' she whispered.

'Good. We will meet up later and discuss what we have learned.'

'You've hardly touched your dinner,' said Sally, looking at the meal Lady Carlton had sent to Catherine's room on a tray. 'You must eat more than that.'

Catherine picked up her fork half-heartedly and toyed with the sole. It was exquisitely prepared by Lady Carlton's French chef, but Catherine had no stomach for it. She applauded Lady Carlton for her tact in offering her guests their meals in their room - news of Miss Simpson's accident had travelled throughout the house, and it seemed somehow disrespectful to take dinner in the dining-room as though nothing had happened. But Catherine could not summon up any appetite.

'It was a dreadful thing to happen,' said Sally sympathetically, having heard all about it in the servants' hall. 'But it isn't like you to go all to pieces,' she observed.

Catherine put down her fork.

'There's something more, isn't there?' asked Sally perceptively.

Catherine nodded slowly. 'Yes.'

'You might as well tell me. It'll only eat away at you if you keep it to yourself.'

Not for the first time, Catherine was glad of the close relationship she had with Sally. She did indeed need to unburden herself. Not until she had done so would she be able to make sense of the strange and disturbing things she had uncovered.

Briefly, she told Sally about her conversation in the library with Mr Stanton, and their agreement to meet up later in the evening to discuss their progress.

'So you think Miss Simpson's death might not have been an accident?' asked Sally.

'I know it wasn't.'

'You know?' Sally looked at her in surprise. 'But you haven't seen Mr Stanton yet. You don't know the cord was cut. It may well just have frayed. Accidents do happen, even to people whose cousins were murdered, you know.'

Catherine's face was expressionless. 'That's true. But you see, when Mr Stanton suggest I go to the stables I followed his advice. And I found something that proves Miss Simpson was murdered.'

'You mean one of the grooms had seen or heard something?' asked Sally, pausing in her act of turning back the bed.

Catherine shook her head. 'No. Miss Simpson did not ride out this morning. She was about to saddle her horse when she suddenly changed her mind. I could not understand it. Why would she suddenly change her mind? Did she see or hear something to put her off the idea? I did not know. So I decided to go out for a ride myself. I felt it would give me time to think.'

'The very idea. Going out for a ride at this time of night,' said Sally. 'If you were a good rider it would be bad enough, but you can't have forgotten the time you fell off your horse and had us all thinking you were dead.'

Catherine couldn't help a smile. 'I was only seven at the time,' she pointed out.

'That's as may be,' said Sally ominously.

'Well, in the event, I didn't go out for a ride. Because, you see, not wanting to trouble the grooms so late in the evening, I collected my saddle myself. But as soon as I picked it up I knew why Miss Simpson had come into my room threatening me with a pistol.'

'You did?' Sally looked at Catherine as though the shock she had received that evening may well have turned her mind.

'I did,' said Catherine resolutely. 'The girth had been cut almost through.'

'What?' Sally's voice was sharp. 'You mean someone had tampered with your saddle?'

Catherine nodded.

'I don't like it,' said Sally with a frown. 'I really don't. I think we should leave here, Miss Catherine, first thing in the morning. It's a bad place. Bad things happen here. Tell Lady Carlton you need some sea air to settle your nerves.'

'I shall do no such thing,' returned Catherine with spirit. 'Besides, although someone has tampered with my saddle it is clear that I was not the intended victim. The intended victim was Miss Simpson.'

'I don't know how you can say such a thing. Why should anyone wanting to harm Miss Simpson tamper with *your* saddle?'

'Because I had offered it to lend it to her,' said Catherine. 'We fell into conversation and she happened to mention that she found Lady Carlton's saddles unforgiving. I told her she might borrow mine.'

'And you're saying someone else knew this?' asked Sally dubiously.

'I made no secret of the offer. Anyone could have overheard. And if they had not overheard me yesterday they could have overheard me this morning. Miss Simpson asked me if she could borrow it and I said yes. The conversation took place in the library, but the windows were open.' As she said it she remembered the three Maltravers girls practising their archery with the Thomas boys. And she remembered Mr Spence passing just beneath the window.

Sally sat down on the bed. 'It does seem to make sense,' she said. 'But still,' she went on more briskly, 'you don't know that cord on the picture was cut. The saddle may have been an accident. Or maybe a piece of malice on the part of a stablehand - someone who's been dismissed, perhaps, over the past few weeks. It may not be connected with Miss Simpson's accident at all.'

Catherine was about to shake her head when she paused. There was, after all, some sense in what Sally said. It was possible that the damage to her saddle had indeed been the work of someone with a grudge against the Carltons - as Sally suggested, a disgruntled stablehand. Or perhaps even a naughty child who had thought of the damage as a joke; something that would give the owner a tumble, perhaps, catapulting them into a muddy ditch.

Yes, it was possible - just possible.

It might not have been intended to do anyone

serious harm. She must not leap to conclusions as Miss Simpson had done - for now she understood the meaning of Miss Simpson's outburst: Miss Simpson, examining the saddle out of interest before going for a ride, had discovered that the girth had been cut, and had realised that if she had been on horseback it would have broken, causing her to fall from her horse.

Knowing that the saddle was Catherine's, she had leapt to the conclusion that Catherine had cut the girth because she wanted to kill her - seemingly then leaping to the further conclusion that Catherine had therefore killed Miss Winter. But why? Lord Amundel had killed Miss Winter? Hadn't he? And Miss Simpson, along with everyone else, must surely have known that?

Catherine shook her head, puzzled. Still, at least the meaning of Miss Simpson's outburst was now somewhat clearer. But Miss Simpson assumptions had been mistaken. She had leapt to a false conclusion, and Catherine knew that she must not fall into the same trap. She must not assume that Miss Simpson's death was murder simply because the unfortunate young lady was now dead. There was a chance that her death was exactly what it seemed, a tragic accident, and nothing more.

'The thing you ought to do is speak to Mr Stanton,' said Sally practically.

Catherine nodded slowly. 'You're right.'

'And to do that you'll need to eat.'

Catherine sighed. She did not really want the sole, even though, under its silver cover, it had kept hot. But Sally was right: she must eat.

She picked at the fish, and managed at last to push

it down.

The house was unusually quiet. Catherine felt self-conscious as she walked down the corridor which housed the bachelor rooms. By rights she should not be in this part of the house. But she needed to see Mr Stanton, and as he was not in any of the rooms downstairs, this was the place she would find him.

She hesitated outside his room. Fortunately she knew which one it was, as she had seen him emerging from it when she had been going downstairs that morning. Even so, she did not like to go in.

But this was silly. She must.

Summoning her courage she knocked at the door.

There was no answer.

She waited a minute and then knocked again.

Still no answer.

What to do?

She did not want to go back to her room with her questions unanswered, but did she really feel capable of going into his room to wait?

She hesitated, then turned the doorknob and went in.

The mellow light of evening cast the room in muted tones. A half-tester bed was pushed back against the wall on her right hand side. On the wall to her left was a fireplace, and beside it a further door. Could he be through there?

She hesitated again. But the further room may be a sitting room, for all she knew, and Mr Stanton could be there, reading a book - he may well have been given a suite of rooms.

She went into the bedroom, feeling her heart

beginning to beat more quickly, and then went over to the further door. She knocked again. No answer. She tried again, and then went in.

The room was a dressing-room. A mahogany washstand stood at one end of it, complete with a plain ewer and bowl. A range of masculine items - brushes and razors - were arranged on the stand. But there was no sign of Mr Stanton.

She was about to leave when something caught her eye: a letter, which had fallen to the floor. Tidiness prompted her to pick it up. As her hand reached out towards it, however, she realised that that would reveal she had invaded his inner sanctum and she decided against it. But just as she paused she caught sight of the direction on the letter. What she saw made her blood run cold.

A sound jolted her into action. Footsteps were walking along the corridor.

Hurriedly she left the dressing-room and as the footsteps halted outside the door she arranged herself hastily in a slipper chair set by the window. She had just settled her skirts when the door opened and Mr Stanton came in.

He did not see her at first, but as he closed the door behind him he caught sight of her. His face broke into an instinctive smile.

'Catherine,' he said.

'Miss Morton,' she corrected him, standing up.

He made her a light bow. 'Of course.'

'I did not mean to intrude —'

'I'm glad you did.'

' — but I could not find you downstairs. And then, when I found your door open, I decided to sit and wait. I hope you don't mind?'

'Mind?' His voice was husky. 'I'm delighted.'

In the dusk he looked more handsome than ever. The fading light threw him into silhouette, accentuating his sculpted features and the strong muscles of his arms and chest.

She felt her heart skip a beat.

But she could not allow herself to have feelings for him. Not after what she had just seen. It would be far too dangerous.

'So,' he said, motioning her to sit down and taking a shield-backed chair for himself. 'What have you discovered?'

Now was the time for her to dissemble. A few short minutes ago she would have told him everything, but the situation had changed. She would need to tread warily. She must be on her guard.

'Very little. Miss Simpson did not go out riding this morning, after all. She went out to the stables, but after telling the grooms she wanted to take Milksocks out she suddenly changed her mind.'

He raised his eyebrows. 'Did you question the grooms about it?'

'Yes. But they did not know why she had changed her mind.' She did not mention the fact that the saddle's girth had been cut, and that Miss Simpson must have noticed it, deciding not to ride as a consequence.

He frowned. 'A pity.'

'And you?' she asked. 'What did you discover?'

'Very little also.' He shifted in his seat, making himself more comfortable, then continued. 'By the time I returned to the bedroom Lord Carlton had already ordered the picture cord replaced. Though the new cord had not yet been fitted, the old one had been taken away. When I discovered this I instructed my valet to make enquiries in the servants' hall, but the cord had been thrown on the gardeners' bonfire. I went out to the bonfire, but the cord was already burning.'

'So now we will never know if the cord was frayed, or if it was cut. Do you know,' said Catherine, glad of the dim light so that he could not clearly see her face, and would not guess that she was being less than truthful, 'I am beginning to think it was the former. It is unlikely that anyone would want to kill Miss Simpson, and even more unlikely that if they wanted to kill her they would try to do it in such an uncertain way.'

'I don't agree. The murderer, if murderer there is, would risk nothing by such a method. They could cut the cord and then simply wait and see what happened. If Miss Simpson was not killed, then nothing would be lost. If she was, they would have gained their ends without drawing suspicion down on themselves. Her death would be put down to an accident. And the murderer would get away scot free.'

'If murderer there is,' said Catherine, repeating his phrase. 'But that is just it. I don't believe there is a murderer.'

'But Miss Simpson's visit to your room?'

'She is - was - a highly strung young woman. Her cousin's death had preyed on her mind, and she had given way to hysteria. She is not the first woman to have had a hysterical outburst, and she won't be the last.'

He gave a sigh. 'You are probably right. You will say nothing, then?'

She shook her head. 'No. I have no wish to stir up any more trouble for Lord and Lady Carlton. Whitegates already has a bad reputation. I will do nothing to fuel it.'

He nodded. 'I agree. It isn't worth making a fuss when there is no proof of foul play.'

Catherine stood up. 'And now I must go,' she said.

He stood up, too.

She was suddenly conscious of how tall he was.

'Good . . . good night,' she said falteringly.

He took her hand and kissed it. A shiver ran through her, from the tips of her fingers to the tips of her toes.

His dark eyes burned into her own. 'Good night,' he said.

Catherine curled herself up in bed, hugging her knees. It had been a disturbing day and she longed to sleep, but sleep would not come. She kept seeing the direction on the letter again in her mind's eye, the direction that had changed her attitude to Mr Stanton - although she was disturbed to find that beneath her fear and distrust a powerful attraction still lay.

What had been the meaning of it? Was there an innocent explanation?

But the more she thought about it, the more she thought it was impossible. What innocent explanation could there be?

She turned over, and began to count sheep.

One, she thought, as a neat white sheep leapt over a stile.

Two. A curly ram followed it.

Three. The next sheep prevaricated and refused to go over the stile. It broke away and ran round the field instead. A sheep dog went to chase it . . .

This is ridiculous, she thought.

She turned over again.

Think of something pleasant. Imagine something wonderful happening. Something good . . .

His head bending down to hers and his arms, wrapping around her waist, holding her tighter. His mouth hovering over her lips and then—

What am I thinking?

She sat bolt upright in bed.

She had been thinking of Mark Stanton taking her in his arms and kissing her - and Mark Stanton was a prime suspect for Miss Simpson's murder.

She could not block it out any further. He had silenced the gardener, so that she would not learn about the original murder; he had been the first person on the scene of Miss Simpson's "accident", not counting herself, but then she had a room only a few doors away from Miss Simpson, whereas his room was at the other end of the house; he had done everything in his power to find out what she knew, and not just what she knew but what she was thinking about the "accident"; and he had had a letter in his dressing-room addressed to Lord Amundel.

Lord Amundel. The man who had supposedly murdered Miss Winter, and who had then shot himself because he was unable to live with the guilt.

How could Mark Stanton have a letter addressed to Lord Amundel?

Unless there had been foul play.

Chapter Seven

'Oh, what a terrible thing to happen. Quite terrible. Truly dreadful, my dear.'

Miss Emmeline Rivers, Lady Cuthbertson's companion, shook her head as she hemmed a handkerchief and unburdened herself to Catherine.

Who does she usually talk to? wondered Catherine with a wave of sympathy; for although Miss Rivers was expected to listen endlessly to Lady Cuthbertson, matching her moods and constantly agreeing with her, she seemed to have no one to turn to herself. So Catherine was glad to provide an outlet for the spinster's worries. A penniless spinster, Catherine thought, is in a difficult position, particularly if she has been gently raised: she cannot set up in business, for society will not allow it, and yet she is still expected to earn her bread. And the only way she can do so is by being at another's beck and call. Not for the first time Catherine silently thanked her father for having left her so well provided for.

'Yes, another tragedy,' said Miss Rivers. 'And following so soon after the first. For although two years may seem like a long time to some people, I declare to me it seems no time at all.'

'You were here when Miss Winter fell to her death?' asked Catherine, hazarding a guess.

'Yes.' Miss Rivers made a gentle tutting noise as again she shook her head. 'Such a lovely young girl. So full of life - Miss Winter, I mean. Of course, Miss Simpson was a lovely young girl too, but quiet, you know. Her cousin wasn't like that. Oh, no, Miss Winter was a lively young woman. And very pretty, my dear. Quite enchanting, in fact.'

Miss Rivers rested her handkerchief in her lap and gazed into the distance, as if remembering Miss Winter. Then again she shook her head. 'So popular, you know, particularly with the gentlemen. There was young Lord Amundel, of course, her fiancé. And then there was Mr Glover. Quite smitten, he was, and you could well see why. Golden hair, she had, curled like an angel's, and the loveliest blue eyes.' Miss Rivers gave a sentimental sigh.

'Mr Glover?' asked Catherine. 'He was here, then, when Miss Winters was killed?'

'Oh, yes, my dear. Distraught, he was. Positively distracted. He was the first to find her, you see. She hadn't come back for dinner and it was young Mr Glover who discovered the body - he had been out for an evening stroll.'

'I see.' Catherine's voice was thoughtful. Mr Glover had been smitten with Miss Winter, and had been the first to find her body. Was her death as clear cut as it had seemed? And what of Miss Simpson? Mr Glover had also been smitten with Miss Simpson, and she too had met with an accident. Could there be a link, Catherine asked herself, or was she reading too much into it?

She did not know. But she was curious to learn more. Realising that Miss Rivers, being for once free of Lady Cuthbertson who was resting in bed with a bad head, was in communicative mood, she decided to find out as much as she could about the house party that had been held at Whitegates two years before. To begin with she ascertained which of the present guests had been present at the earlier party and then returned to the subject of Mr Glover.

'It must have been very distressing for Mr Glover,' she remarked.

'Yes.' Miss Rivers sighed. 'He was very upset.'

'And it must also have been upsetting for you, of course,' said Catherine. 'Being in the same house at the time,' she explained.

Miss Rivers' glasses misted over at being shown any form of consideration, something she was completely unused to. 'Well, it wasn't very pleasant,' she admitted. 'But then, it was even worse for Elaine.'

'Elaine?'

'Lady Cuthbertson, I mean,' said Miss River, flustered. 'Pray, my dear, do not tell her I used her Christian name. It was only a slip of the moment. I would not like to offend her, not after all she has done for me.'

'You have been her companion since her marriage?' asked Catherine, hazarding another guess.

Miss Rivers nodded. 'Such a good thing for her. A wonderful marriage, for she was quite penniless, you know.' She gave another sentimental sigh, and just for a moment a smile played about her lips, as though she was thinking that if one penniless lady could marry well, then perhaps another might do the same. 'Quite like a fairytale it was. We were at school together, you know.'

Catherine was startled. She had thought Lady Cuthbertson and Miss Rivers came from completely different walks of life but it seemed she was wrong.

'She was always a bright girl, even then. "Miss Fanshaw, you will go far," our dear headmistress used to say. Whereas I was not very bright, you know. Though I was always good at needlework,' she added, looking with pride at the neat stitching that lined the handkerchief. 'And, of course, that has been of great value to Lady Cuthbertson. I am able to do all her fancy sewing for her, and I am adept at embroidery as well.'

'That must be useful,' said Catherine kindly.

'Yes, you know, it is.'

Miss Rivers turned her attention back to her sewing, her long, slender fingers stitching neatly and evenly.

'How did Lord and Lady Cuthbertson meet?' asked Catherine. She realised that she knew very little about the womanish Lord Cuthbertson, and if she was to consider Miss Simpson's death in the light of a possible murder she knew she must discover as much as she could about each of her fellow guests - particularly those who had been at the house party two years before when Miss Winter had been killed.

'Oh, it was so romantic!' Miss Rivers gave another sentimental sigh. 'Elaine was the governess to little Johnny, Lord Cuthbertson's brother - a strange thing, for although they were brothers, or perhaps I should say half brothers, little Johnny was forty years younger then Lord Cuthbertson. So you see he needed a governess to look after the boy. Well, Elaine was always accomplished, of course, and she was offered the position. A lovely position it was at that, looking after a dear little boy at Lord Cuthbertson's country seat - Moorfield, in Staffordshire. Do you know it?'

'No. I have never been to Staffordshire.'

'Parts of it are wild. I found it just a little daunting when first I went there. But of course I soon became used to it, and grew to love the walks: Lady Cuthbertson is a great walker. Well, you know, Elaine was devoted to little Johnny, and Lord Cuthbertson was so grateful to her for everything she did. It is hardly surprising that he fell in love with her. Propinquity, you know, that is what it is. And then of course he married her.'

She fell silent, once again seemingly lost in a day dream.

Then, rousing herself, she continued. 'And then she thought of me.' Her face expressed her humble gratitude. 'And really, it is an excellent position. For although I have some skill with a needle, I was finding life rather hard. She gave me a position as her companion, you see, and I have lived with her at Moorfield ever since.'

'A very satisfactory arrangement for both of you, I am sure,' said Catherine.

'Yes, indeed.'

'Lord Cuthbertson seems a perfect gentleman,' observed Catherine, as the conversation had wandered back to the subject of Miss Rivers' gratitude to Lady Cuthbertson, instead of the more interesting subject of Lord Cuthbertson.

'Yes, indeed. Most gentlemanlike,' said Miss Rivers firmly.

Rather too firmly, thought Catherine. Was there

something disreputable in Lord Cuthbertson's past? she wondered.

Really, I am imagining things, she reprimanded herself firmly. If I am to do any good I must confine myself strictly to the facts.

'Does he spend the year in Staffordshire, or does he spend part of his time in London?'

Miss Rivers shook her head. 'No. He does not like London. And Lady Cuthbertson feels the same. I must say I think I would find it enjoyable,' she added rather wistfully. 'But it is noisy, Lord Cuthbertson says, and dirty, and crowded. Lord Cuthbertson prefers to remain on his estate. He does not like crowds.'

'He does not have any business to attend to, then?' asked Catherine.

'No.' Miss Rivers sighed, as though thinking it a pity. Business would take him to London, and where he went his wife would surely follow. And where she went, Miss Rivers would go. 'He only accepted the invitation to Whitegates because he and Lord Carlton share an interest in old books,' she said.

'His family must have been pleased at his marriage,' observed Catherine.

'Oh, no. That is, he has no family. Not any more.'

Catherine was about to enquire further into this promising revelation when the door opened and Lord Carlton walked in.

'But I had better go upstairs and see if Lady Cuthbertson needs anything,' said Miss Rivers, recalled to her position by the interruption. 'It is such a trial to have a sore head.'

Gathering up her needlework in her fine hands she bustled out of the room.

'Ah! Catherine. Just the person I was looking for,' said Lord Carlton. 'Will you favour me with a game of chess?'

Catherine agreed readily to his proposal, and after an interesting game which she unfortunately lost she returned to her room. As she did so she thought over everything she had learnt. She had learnt that Miss Rivers was endlessly grateful to her old school friend for giving her a position; that Lord Cuthbertson was a perfect gentleman who didn't like noise or crowds . . . and that Mr Glover had had a passion for two young ladies who had both ended up in early graves.

Catherine was sitting at the writing-table in her room. The case was becoming perplexing and she decided that writing down what she had learnt might help her make sense of it. She took a sheet of paper out of one of the drawers then, dipping her quill into the ink she began to write.

She started by making a list of all the people who were staying at Whitegates Manor, and next to their names she wrote the following notes:

Mr Stanton - presence prevented the gardener from talking about Miss Winter's murder; first at the scene of Miss Simpson's accident; in possession of a letter addressed to Lord Amundel. Not present at the Manor two years ago when Miss Winter murdered

Mr Glover - besotted with Miss Winter and Miss Simpson, both of whom are now dead. Present at the Manor two years ago

Lord Cuthbertson - a perfect gentleman? Dislikes crowds and noise. No longer has any family. Present at the Manor two years ago

---

Lady Cuthbertson - present at the Manor two years ago

Miss Emmeline Rivers - present at the Manor two years ago

The Thomas boys - not present at the Manor two years ago

Mrs Maltravers and her daughters - not present at the Manor two years ago

Lord Gilstead - present at the Manor two years ago

Mr Edmund Spence - walking past the window when Miss Simpson asked to borrow my saddle; though I had already made the offer the previous day when anyone could have heard. Not present at the Manor two years ago

She read through the list and then, unwillingly, added

Lady Carlton - hosted both parties

Lord Carlton - hosted both parties. Saw to the burning of the picture cord. Now impossible to tell whether or not it was cut

She sanded the list and then read it through again. So far it seemed that Mr Stanton, Mr Glover and Lord Carlton were the likeliest suspects, if indeed Miss Simpson's death was a case of murder and not a genuine accident: although Mr Stanton had not been present two years previously when Miss Winter had met her death.

The thought gave Catherine some relief.

Could it have been an accident? She stroked the end of her quill against her cheek thoughtfully: she would know more on that score when she had had a chance to speak to Sally. The redoubtable maid was making discreet enquiries in the servants' hall to find out whether or not there had been any disgruntled grooms or servants dismissed from the Manor recently, anyone who may have a grudge against the Carltons. And she was also trying to discover whether there were any mischievous children in the neighbourhood who may have cut through the girth of her saddle without realising that the prank could prove fatal.

As Catherine thought again of the cut girth she inclined more to the idea that Miss Simpson's death had indeed been murder. One accident was possible, but two - and if Miss Simpson had gone out riding then the cut girth would inevitably have caused a nasty accident - in so short a space of time, and happening to the same person, were highly unlikely.

She put down her quill and then, seeing that the ink was dry, she folded the list and tucked it away in her reticule.

'But I don't see *why*.'

Miss Maltravers was pouting as Catherine walked out into the gardens and straight into the middle of an argument.

'Because it isn't seemly,' said Mrs Maltravers, who for once seemed not to be on her giddy daughters' side. 'Miss Simpson's body has only just left the house. You can't possibly rehearse another one of Mr Spence's plays.'

'This is no ordinary play,' said Mr Spence in a suitably grave manner. 'This is to be my master work. *The Tragedy of the Innocent*, or *Death at Whitegates Manor*.'

'No,' said Mrs Maltravers. 'It's out of the question.'

'But I'm to play Miss Simpson,' pleaded Clarissa. 'It's the leading part.'

'I cannot see why you would want to play such an unfortunate part,' said Mrs Maltravers.

'But —'

'No. My mind is made up. And you, Mr Spence, pray do not encourage her. I have no doubt of your talents —'

'Believe me, dear lady, this is the play that will make my name. The double tragedy will undoubtedly create attention, and a play dealing with it will be sponsored without a doubt. I expect to see it performed at Drury Lane.'

'But not, I think, with Miss Clarissa taking the leading part.'

And so saying, Mrs Maltravers gathered together her three protesting daughters and hustled them into the house.

'You are dedicated to your work,' said Catherine thoughtfully, as Mr Spence turned towards her.

'An artist has no choice,' he replied dramatically.

'Do you really think the play will attract a sponsor?'

'There is no doubt about it. Romantic tragedies have always been popular, and this one has the benefit of being true.'

'How far would you go to gain a sponsor for your play?' asked Catherine.

Something wary entered Mr Spence's eye, and Catherine realised she had blundered. Her question had been too direct, and if Mr Spence was responsible for the tragedy would put him on his guard. Thinking quickly, she said, 'I know of a rich gentleman in Scotland who may be persuaded to put some money into an artistic enterprise.'

'Ah! I see. That is what you meant by how far. Scotland is quite a way,' he said thoughtfully, then shook his head. 'No. I don't believe I need go so far. The money will come from London, I am convinced. Now, if I can only get Kean to play the lead part . . . '

Catherine was surprised. 'Will the lead part not go to a woman? I know that Sarah Siddons has retired, but there are other accomplished actresses . . . surely it is the part of Miss Simpson that will be the leading rôle?'

'Miss Simpson?' He looked genuinely surprised. 'My dear Miss Morton, it is the part of the playwright that will take centre stage.'

Catherine looked at him in amazement. Surely his vanity was not so great that he saw himself as being the major player in the drama. Unless . . . But no, that was absurd. Not even Mr Spence's vanity could lead him to write a play about a murder he had committed, with the playwright - the murderer? - being given the main rôle. Could he?

But then, how much about Mr Spence did she really know?

By the end of the afternoon her head was spinning. She longed to be alone. Every time she spoke to one of her fellow guests she found herself reading double meanings into everything they said. She had suspected each and every one of them of killing Miss Winter and Miss Simpson during the course of the day, and she needed a rest.

Her wanderings led her unknowingly towards the lake.

She was just about to sit down when the glint of water through the trees caught her eye, and she decided to sit by the water a while before returning to the house.

She followed a path through the trees and came out not far from a natural beach. She looked out across the lake. Its blue surface was smooth and unruffled. And then she saw something . . . a man's head and torso rising from the depths. Tanned and lean and muscular, the sight took her breath away. It was Mr Stanton, swimming naked in the lake.

She should look away. She should run back to her room overcome with maidenly modesty. But she stood transfixed. His body was so different from her own, covered in ridges of hard muscles where her own was full and soft, and so beautiful. As the sunlight caught on the droplets of water clinging to him he turned slightly and, lifting his arms, ran his strong hands through his wet hair. Rivulets of water ran over his shoulder and down his back. Then, with a quick, sure movement, he dived beneath the water again, his head disappearing and his loins and legs surfacing briefly as he flicked himself down into the depths.

Catherine stood watching the spot where he had been, feeling weak at the knees.

Why did he have to have this effect on her? He was one of the prime suspects in the murder of Miss Simpson and yet he turned her insides to molten wax.

Life was indeed a jester, she thought.

She just hoped her attraction to Mr Stanton would

not turn out to be one of its crueller jokes.

Chapter Eight

'These are the people who visited the stables after you offered Miss Simpson your saddle and before she went out to the stables herself,' said Sally the following morning. 'I took the liberty of asking the grooms whilst I was out there.'

'Well done.' Catherine took the list, which was made out in Sally's large but even hand. She glanced at the names: Mr Spence, Lady Cuthbertson, Mrs Maltravers and Lord Gilstead. 'A mixed group,' she said. 'How did you get on with finding out if Lord Carlton has had problems with any disgruntled servants?'

'Nothing,' said Sally, shaking her head. 'Lord Carlton's a good master, by all accounts. No disgruntled servants, no one with a grudge. And no mischievous children either.'

Catherine sighed. 'Do you know, Sally, I was hoping there would be? That Miss Simpson's death was an unfortunate accident, and that the damage to my saddle was done without evil intent.'

'And why would you wish that?' asked Sally innocently.

'Isn't it obvious?' Catherine spoke defensively. 'Murder is an unpleasant thing,'

'It is. Especially if it is committed by a handsome

bachelor,' Sally remarked.

Catherine sighed. She should rebuke Sally for impertinence but she did not have the heart to do it.

'But I did find something interesting,' said Sally. 'Something about Mrs Maltravers.'

'Mrs Maltravers was not here two years ago,' said Catherine. 'And besides, what possible motive could she have had?'

'She may not have been here at Whitegates, but she was in the area. She was staying with her cousin at Bellcroft Lodge, and that's less than twenty minutes away. What's more, she *did* have a motive, at least for wishing Miss Winter ill. She wanted Lord Amundel to marry Clarissa, you see.'

'She wanted Lord Amundel to marry her oldest daughter?' asked Catherine in surprise.

'Yes.' Sally nodded vigorously. 'Apparently Clarissa had seen a lot of Lord Amundel in London. They had danced together any number of times, and they'd kept bumping into each other at the theatre and the like. Clarissa was very keen on him and he seemed keen on her. "Keen as mustard," the housekeeper says.'

'And how would she know?' asked Catherine curiously.

'She's friendly with the housekeeper at Bellcroft Lodge. All Miss Maltravers' relations were delighted. Think of it - their Clarissa marrying a lord. Mrs Maltravers did all she could to push things along. That's why she got her cousin to invite her and the girls down to the Lodge. So she could throw Clarissa in Lord Amundel's way.'

'But instead he fell in love with Miss Winter,' said

Catherine thoughtfully. 'And they became engaged. Most likely he had been in love with her for some time, and the Maltravers had simply misjudged the strength of his attraction to Clarissa. But if something had happened to Miss Winter - ' She shook her head impatiently. 'No. Lord Amundel would not have transferred his affections to Miss Maltravers just because Miss Winter was dead.'

'Not at first, maybe,' said Sally. 'But who knows? In time. If he was grief-stricken and Miss Maltravers comforted him . . . That's the way it happened with Lord and Lady Cuthbertson.'

Catherine looked startled at the conclusion to this sentence.

'Lord Cuthbertson was grief-stricken when his little brother died. Lady Cuthbertson - although of course she wasn't Lady Cuthbertson at that time - comforted him. He was grateful to her to her and the long and the short of it is that he ended up proposing.'

'But Mrs Maltravers did not know that,' pointed out Catherine. 'Lord and Lady Cuthbertson rarely move out of Staffordshire, from what I can gather, and I think it unlikely that Mrs Maltravers would go so far north. She cannot have known about Lord and Lady Cuthbertson's marriage.'

'They may not have bumped into each other before, but Mrs Maltravers may well have heard the story.'

Catherine was about to protest when she paused. Miss Rivers was very voluble on occasion, and may well have told the story of Lady Cuthbertson's marriage to guests at the Manor two years before. And Bellcroft Lodge was only twenty minutes away. The servants at the two houses knew each other, and the story may well have been passed on. In fact, given its romantic nature, it was not only possible that it had been passed on, but probable.

'And maybe Mrs Maltravers thought if grief made Lord Cuthbertson propose to his brother's governess, then why shouldn't grief make Lord Amundel propose to a pretty young woman who comforted him in a grief of his own,' Sally finished.

'And one for whom he had already shown signs of partiality,' said Catherine thoughtfully. 'Even so,' she said more briskly,' that would mean Mrs Maltravers murdering Miss Winter, and I cannot see her going to those lengths to get her daughters off her hands. Particularly as her daughters are pretty and lively. Sooner or later they will get husbands, without their mother having recourse to murder.'

'But will those husbands be titled and rich?'

'Rich.' Catherine thought. 'If Mrs Maltravers was in need of money at the time . . . ' She considered. 'Perhaps I ought to make an effort to find out.'

Having told Catherine everything she had discovered, Sally went into the dressing-room to see to Catherine's clothes.

Left alone, Catherine took her list out of her reticule and added the information Sally had discovered:

Mrs Maltravers and her daughters - not present at the Manor two years ago.

She added, *but staying at Bellcroft Lodge. Mrs Maltravers was in the stables at the right time and could have damaged my saddle. She wanted Lord Amundel to marry her daughter, Clarissa.*

Catherine paused and then made a new entry.

Clarissa? Could she have had a similar idea. More likely candidate than her mother, perhaps? The child is silly and immature? Could she have heard the story of Lord and Lady Cuthbertson's marriage and decided the same thing might work for her?

Lord Gilstead - present at the Manor two years ago. She added, *Also visited the stables on the morning of Miss Simpson's ride.*

Mr Edmund Spence. She read through the entry and added, *Keen to have a play at Drury Lane? Present in the stables and could have damaged the saddle.*

She sat back and looked at the list with a sigh. 'It seems to be getting more complicated, not clearer,' she said.

Sally, coming back into the bedroom, nodded. 'Why don't you give it up?' she said. 'It's not your place to do anything about it, after all. If Lord Carlton's satisfied it was an accident and Miss Simpson's family are satisfied it was an accident . . . why stir things up?'

Catherine felt a great weariness stealing over her. Sally was right. By probing into the matter she was in danger of making life difficult for everyone concerned. If she had had proof that Miss Simpson had been murdered it would have been different. But there was no proof. Could she really justify stirring everything up because she had an idea?

She thought of Lord and Lady Carlton, whom she had known since her earliest years. Life was hard enough for them anyway, as people still connected

Whitegates Manor with Miss Winter's death. It would be even harder for them now that Miss Simpson had died as well. Why should she make things worse by assuming Miss Simpson's death had been murder? No, she could not justify it.

She put the list in the bottom of her valise. 'You're right, Sally. I have become carried away. Better to let Miss Winter and Miss Simpson rest in peace.'

Sally nodded. 'Why not cut your visit short?' she suggested.

'No. I can't do that. I owe it to Lord and Lady Carlton to stay for the allotted time. If I stay, others may do the same. The less scandal that attaches to the house party the better. If an unfortunate accident occurred but everything else went according to plan there will be less of a scandal. Whatever else I do or don't do, I intend to stay until the end of the month.'

'Then in that case,' said Sally, 'I'd better get on with the ironing.'

Catherine felt better once she had taken the decision to abandon the hunt for Miss Simpson's possible murderer. She was tired of seeing her fellow guests in the rôle of cold-blooded killer and wanted, if not to enjoy the rest of the party, at least experience it in peace.

It was in a calmer mood, therefore, that she went downstairs for lunch.

The other guests, she noticed, had adopted more sombre clothing, as she herself had done Although it would not have been appropriate for her to wear black, as she had not been related to Miss Simpson, nevertheless she had donned a sombre gown, and she saw that most of the other ladies were wearing darker shades. Lady Carlton herself was wearing a gown of purple silk.

'You will all be pleased to hear, I am sure, that Miss Simpson's body is being returned to her home for burial. Her chaperon is to travel with her, of course, and her father is to meet them on the road.'

There were murmurs of sympathy and understanding. All the same, the mood lifted a little. Though everyone was sorry for the dead girl and her family, it was a relief to have the incident over with. Now, perhaps, things could begin to return to normal.

Lord and Lady Carlton worked hard over lunch. They introduced a number of unexceptionable topics of conversation and were rewarded by an effort on the part of their guests. By and by the constrained atmosphere left the group, and although the meal could not be said to be jolly, it was at least not morbid.

Afterwards, when the guests broke into small groups, the younger ones going out into the gardens to practise their archery and the older ones to stroll around the grounds, Lady Carlton sought Catherine out.

'It is such a relief to have the worst behind us,' she said. 'For one terrible thing to happen here was bad enough, but for two . . . I don't think Hugh will ever get over it.'

Catherine followed her eyes to where Lord Carlton was conversing with Lord Gilstead. His voice was cheerful, but his shoulders were tense and he kept shifting his stance as though not at ease.

'No blame can attach to you,' said Catherine.

'Of course not. But even so, people talk. First Miss

Winter's death, and now Miss Simpson's. My only consolation is that poor Lord Amundel did not shoot himself here as well. And there is so much to do. I have promised to pack up Miss Simpson's things. Her chaperon was too upset, poor woman, and as haste was of the essence I encouraged her to leave as soon as she was ready, promising I would pack Miss Simpson's boxes and send them on. I cannot do it now, however. I want to pay as much attention as I can to my guests. They have had a shock, and it is my duty as their hostess to make them as comfortable as possible. And I must confess I have selfish reasons, too. If I can smooth things over they may stay, and there will be less cause for scandal and gossip if things proceed as planned. But still . . . ' She hesitated. 'May I ask you a favour?'

'Of course.'

'Will you lock Miss Simpson's room for me? I meant to do it earlier - I don't want any of the servants going in there for ghoulish thrills, or the next thing I know they will be giving in their notice, saying they have seen her ghost.' She cast an anxious glance at her husband, obviously wanting to go over to him and give him her moral support.

'I'll do it now,' said Catherine.

'Thank you, my dear.' Lady Carlton's gratitude was heartfelt.

She handed Catherine the key, then went over to Lord Carlton, placing her hand on his arm and joining in with his conversation, devoting her energies to setting her guests at ease.

Catherine walked down the corridor, feeling a racing

of her heart. Her memories were not pleasant. The last time she had walked down this corridor she had found something gruesome at the end of it. There was nothing there now, however, she reminded herself, but an empty room. She straightened her shoulders and continued.

She drew closer to Miss Simpson's room - then stopped.

No, she couldn't have. She must have imagined it. She couldn't possibly have heard something. There could not be noises coming from the dead girl's room. Could there?

She listened.

Nothing.

She went on.

Cautiously she went into the room . . . to find a hand clamped over her mouth and a strong arm pulling her backwards, behind the door. And then someone swung her round.

'What are - what the hell!' The exclamation was wrung from Catherine's assailant as sharp teeth bit into his hand and abruptly he let go.

Catherine threw herself across the room, poised ready for flight . .. before registering that the man who had so frighteningly caught hold of her was none other than Mark Stanton.

'What are you doing here?' she demanded, her heart racing, her body balanced on the balls of her feet, ready to fly at a moment's notice.

'I might ask you the same question,' he said, taking a large white linen handkerchief out of his pocket and with a 'Damn!' wrapping it round his bloodied hand.

'*I* am here at Lady Carlton's request.'

'Are you indeed?'

'I am,' she said, chest heaving.

'Whereas I am here for nefarious purposes, I suppose.'

She did not miss the acid note in his voice.

'If you are not, then why did you attack me?'

'Hardly an attack,' he said, tucking the ends of his handkerchief under the makeshift bandage. 'And a sensible precaution under the circumstances.'

'The circumstances being?'

'That someone was approaching a murdered young woman's room in a furtive manner.'

'I was not furtive!'

'You will allow me to tell you that you were,' he said severely. 'Your footsteps were hesitant, and at one point stopped altogether.'

'That was because I heard noises!'

He stopped what he was doing, his hand pausing as he finished the bandage. 'I didn't make a sound!'

'You were making a noise like a herd of elephants,' Catherine said defiantly.

The remark was so ridiculous that a moment later they were both laughing, despite their best efforts to do nothing of the kind.

'And you, of course, know what a herd of elephants sounds like,' said Mr Stanton, with a raise of his dark eyebrows.

'I am well acquainted with the sound,' said Catherine, a mischievous twitch at the corner of her mouth.

He laughed heartily. Then, controlling his mirth, he said, 'But come. Tell me. What are you doing here,

Miss Morton, at Lady Carlton's request?'

'I am locking up Miss Simpson's room.'

'Ah. So that's it. Well, it's a wise precaution, if it's come a little late. Nothing must be disturbed. Lady Carlton realises, then, that it is a case of murder?'

'She realises nothing of the kind. Indeed, I don't believe it myself. I can see no reason why anyone would murder Miss Simpson.'

'That is not what you felt before.'

'I let my imagination get out of hand.'

He regarded her thoughtfully. 'You are not being honest with me.'

'A most ungentlemanlike thing to say,' she remarked, fencing with him.

'Perhaps. But it is true, all the same.'

She felt uncomfortable. Unconsciously, she clasped her hands together and wrung them slightly.

'What is it, Catherine? Why are you not being honest with me?'

Once again he was having a strange effect on her. His voice was so husky that it seemed to reverberate inside her in all the most inconvenient places. She longed to tell him what she really felt, but there was so much about him she did not know. So much about him she did not trust. Except, that was not strictly true. On an instinctive level she felt she could trust him absolutely. But there were too many unaccountable things in his behaviour for her to feel completely at ease.

'It started when you were in my room,' he said, appearing to cast his mind back. 'You were ill at ease. I felt then you were not being open with me but I put it down to our surroundings. For a gently raised young lady to find herself alone in a gentleman's bedroom - particularly when such a strong attraction exists between us - well, I could understand your reaction. Or thought I could. But now I am beginning to think there is something more.'

Catherine hesitated. Then, slowly, she spoke. 'You do realise, that if Miss Simpson was murdered, you would be a likely suspect?'

'I?' He was genuinely startled.

She nodded. 'Your presence prevented the gardener telling me about Miss Winter's death. You were the first person to arrive at Miss Simpson's room after myself, despite the fact your room is at the other end of the house. And —'

'And?' he queried.

'Don't you think that is enough?'

'You do realise that, if I am the murderer, you have just signed your death warrant?' he asked. 'I am larger than you . . . faster . . . stronger . . . Are you not afraid?'

Catherine let out a long sigh. 'No. I don't know why, but I'm not.'

'Then you are either very brave or very foolish,' he said thoughtfully. 'Confronting a man with the knowledge that you believe him to be a murderer . .. '

'I didn't say I believed you to be a murderer.' Although if she had allowed herself to be ruled by her head she might well have done so. 'I merely said you were a likely suspect.'

He sat down on the edge of the writing-table, folding his arms and stretching his legs out in front of him. 'Because I didn't want the gardener to upset you? And because I was on my way down to dinner, and therefore close to Miss Simpson's room, when the maid let out her blood-curdling scream?'

'And because . . . '

'Yes?'

'And because there was a letter in your dressing-room addressed to Lord Amundel.'

There was a sudden silence. Outside, the birds were still singing, and in the distance a door banged. But inside the room everything was unnaturally still.

Have I been foolish? Catherine asked herself, suddenly afraid. Have I trusted my instincts to the detriment of my own safety?

She held her breath.

And then let it out again as he made no move to attack her but instead began to speak.

'That was unexpected,' he said with a frown. 'I did not know you had been in my dressing-room.'

'I took care you should not know.'

'There is a very good reason why I had a letter addressed to Lord Amundel in my dressing-room.' He looked her straight in the eye. 'You see, I *am* Lord Amundel.'

Catherine was stunned. Before she had realised what she was doing she had sunk into a chair. She sat there momentarily bereft of speech.

Lord Amundel? Mr Stanton was Lord Amundel?

'But that's impossible,' she said. 'Lord Amundel is dead.'

He answered her obliquely. 'The King is dead. Long live the King.'

Catherine looked at him, searching his face as though she would find the answer written there. And as his words began to sink in she realised what he was telling her. 'The King is dead. Long live the King.' She looked at him in sudden understanding. 'When a man dies his title does not die with him, it simply moves to someone else. Then you . . . you must have been Lord Amundel's heir.'

'Yes.'

She looked at him closely, her eyes running over the sharply defined cheekbones, the firm chin, the smooth brow. 'Lord Amundel was not married - and of course he was too young to have had a son, at least of your age. You were . . . his brother, then?'

'Yes.'

The simplicity of his answer carried more weight than explanations would have done.

So Mr Stanton was Lord Amundel's brother. The tragedy to him was not general, it was personal. 'I'm sorry,' she said.

'So am I.'

She wanted to go to him, to run her hands over his face and to look into his eyes, but convention forbade it. And so she folded her hands in her lap and crossed her feet at the ankle.

He was speaking again. 'Miss Morton, we have a lot to talk about. But I think it best if we do not do it here. The atmosphere is hardly prepossessing. Besides, we may be disturbed. Will you meet me by the lake in an hour?'

'An hour?' She thought of the lake, and her mind replayed the memory of his tanned and muscular chest, followed by the sleek vision of his firm loins and thighs, as he had gracefully flipped himself over and dived under the water.

'Is anything wrong?' he asked, seeing her shiver.

'N . . . no.'

'You will meet me, then?'

She hesitated. She felt instinctively that she could trust him, it was true, but her instincts where he was concerned were clouded. She wanted so much to be near him, to smell the scent of him, to hear his voice, to imagine his touch, that she could not trust her own judgement. And to meet him down by the lake, when she knew that even now there was a possibility he was a murderer, would be foolish indeed. And so she said. 'Not by the lake. But in the library.'

'We will not be so private there - or perhaps that is what you are afraid of.'

'Afraid? I'm not afraid.'

'Aren't you, Catherine?'

He crossed the room until he was standing in front of her. Then he took her hand and raised her to her feet.

She could feel herself leaning towards him. The yearning to be in his arms was so strong that unconsciously she took a step towards him, and her body touched his. A trembling ran through her, and without thinking what she was doing she turned up her face for his kiss. She felt his breath on her lips, and then he covered her mouth with his own.

It was the most marvellous sensation she had ever experienced. It filled every part of her. Her arms snaked around his neck and her fingers tangled themselves in the thickness of his dark hair, pulling his mouth against her own.

His hands slid downwards, coming to rest in the small of her back, and she felt him press her closer. She gasped as a new shiver shot through her, far more primal than the one before.

And then she felt something of his pressure lessen, and realised he was ending the kiss. And then sanity returned. What was she doing, an unmarried and chaste young woman, kissing a man she barely knew?

'No,' he said, looking deep into her eyes, 'you are not.'

His words brought her back to her senses. What had they been discussing? A meeting. Yes, that was it. A meeting by the lake. Or rather in the library. Somewhere with large windows, where it would be almost impossible for him to murder her if he was not what he seemed - although after the kiss she was even more convinced he could never do such a thing.

'In the library, then?' she asked.

He nodded. 'In the library. One hour.' He made her a slight bow and went out of the room. Leaving Catherine to follow, locking the door behind her.

She was about to return to her own room when she saw Lady Carlton coming towards her.

'My dear, thank you. I should not have left you to come here alone. Hugh was quite cross with me when I told him. So I have come to make sure you are not overcome - Hugh tells me he can manage quite well without me.'

Catherine gave a slight smile. 'No. I am not overcome.' Or at least not by memories of Miss Simpson, she thought.

'Could that have anything to do with the fact that Mr Stanton was here?' asked Lady Carlton innocently.

'How -?'

'I saw him leaving the room just before you. My dear, I don't want to interfere - what am I saying? Of course I want to interfere! I am so happy to see you together. I think he would be the very husband for you.'

'Why does everyone keep trying to find me a husband?' asked Catherine with a sigh.

'Because they care about you. And they know that, no matter how nice it is to be free, there are advantages attached to the married state that no single young lady can begin to imagine.'

Oh, I can imagine them, thought Catherine, as the memory of Mr Stanton's kiss still lingered on her lips. Before reminding herself that Lady Carlton had not meant any such thing. She had meant the advantages of a name and social position, and children, perhaps.

'And so, what were you talking about?'

Catherine frowned, wondering how much to say. But she decided there was no harm in letting Lady Carlton know Mr Stanton's true identity - although for some reason he himself had chosen to keep it secret. 'We were talking about his brother.'

'Dear me, I didn't know he had a brother, or I would have invited him here as well.'

'That's just the thing. You did invite him. Two years ago. Lord Amundel was Mr Stanton's brother.'

'Lord Amundel?' Lady Carlton was startled. 'But that means —'

'That Mr Stanton is the new Lord Amundel? Yes, it does.'

'But, my dear, this is wonderful. Not that Lord Amundel is dead - the other Lord Amundel, I mean, Mr Stanton's brother; except he isn't Mr Stanton, or rather he is Mr Stanton, but he is also the Earl of Amundel . . . This is all very confusing, but you know what I mean - but this is a wonderful thing for you.'

'For me?' asked Catherine, surprised.

'Of course. Now that he has inherited the title, the new Lord Amundel will need an heir. And to get one he must marry. If you are sensible, you will turn that fact to your advantage. Now don't frown at me, Catherine. There is nothing like grief and the need for an heir to turn a man's thoughts to matrimony. Look at Lord Cuthbertson. As happy a bachelor as ever there was, with a younger brother - only five years old, courtesy of his father's second wife - to be his heir. Then tragedy strikes. His brother is drowned. He consoles the governess, and she in her turn consoles him. Before you know it they are man and wife.'

Lady Cuthbertson's marriage seems to have inspired every spinster and every matchmaker who has heard of it, thought Catherine wryly. First Miss Rivers, then Mrs Maltravers and now Lady Carlton - all very different ladies, but either unmarried themselves or with unmarried daughters or friends whom they wanted to see wed.

'And really,' Lady Carlton went on, 'why should you not do the same?'

'Do?' queried Catherine. 'I was not aware that Lady Cuthbertson "did" anything.'

'My dear, she must have encouraged him, I'm sure, or he'd never have made a move: Lord Cuthbertson is not the most decisive of men. But why should she not encourage him? Being a governess is not a pleasant life. No one can blame her for trying to improve on her position. Besides, the marriage was a good thing on both sides. She acquired an establishment and Lord Cuthbertson acquired a wife.

And though Lady Cuthbertson may be a martinet she is still of childbearing years. You see, my dear, a most agreeable situation all round.'

'I have no intention of setting my cap at Lord Amundel,' said Catherine firmly. 'And even if I had, I think you will find he is not a man to be coerced. He is not like Lord Cuthbertson. He has a mind of his own.'

'A pity,' said Lady Carlton with a sigh.

'A pity I won't set my cap at him, or a pity he has a mind of his own?' asked Catherine, amused.

Lady Carlton matched her mischievous tone. 'Both!'

Catherine thought better of telling Lady Carlton about her forthcoming meeting with Lord Amundel. She had had enough teasing on the subject of matrimony for one day. 'I would appreciate it if you did not mention his true identity to anyone else,' she said.

Lady Carlton looked surprised.

'I believe he does not want it generally known.'

Lady Carlton looked at her curiously for a minute, but then said, 'Very well.' She thought for a minute and went on, 'I suppose he doesn't want people asking him about his brother's tragic death. Either that, or he doesn't want to be pestered by the Maltravers girls. If their mother once finds out he is a lord they will give him no peace. You may rely on me.'

Catherine was grateful to Lady Carlton for her understanding. Then, feeling that they had talked of Lord Amundel enough, she turned the conversation into less disturbing channels.

'You're going to meet Lord Amundel? I don't know,

miss. Are you sure it's wise?'

Sally spoke dubiously. She had heard all about Mr Stanton's true identity from Catherine and she was concerned.

'I don't know.' Catherine admitted it freely. 'But nevertheless, I am going to keep my appointment with him. I wanted you to know, though, Sally - just in case.'

Deep down, Catherine felt she could trust Lord Amundel, but she was not blind to the fact that he had lied to her about his identity, and that he had been in the dead girl's room.

'Just in case you're murdered, you mean?' asked Sally dourly.

'No, of course not - well, yes.'

'Very well, Miss, if you're murdered I'll tell Lord Carlton it was Lord Amundel who did it. But what good you think that'll do you once you're dead I'm sure I don't know,' she said with a harumph.

'I don't think it will come to that —'

'That's a mercy,' said Sally dryly.

' — and I need to know what Lord Amundel has to say.'

Sally turned away and began folding Catherine's undergarments. 'But would you still need to know what he had to say if he was sixty-five, balding, and missing his teeth?' Sally muttered under her breath.

'I heard that,' said Catherine. 'And yes, I would.'

'Very good, Miss,' said Sally stolidly. 'Just whatever you say.'

Chapter Nine

The clock in the hall struck as Catherine went downstairs. She still had half an hour before she was due to meet Lord Amundel. Her nerves were overstretched and the idea of some fresh air was very appealing. She went out into the gardens and turned her steps towards the shrubbery, where she hoped she would not be disturbed.

The shrubbery was, like the rest of the gardens, well tended, and Catherine enjoyed walking through the cool green shadows. She emerged again soon afterwards, judging it to be time to meet Lord Amundel. As she did so she caught sight of a man and a woman on the lawns. The man she recognised as Lord Gilstead, but who was the woman? Not one of the guests. On the contrary, by the look of her she was a different class of woman altogether. Surely Lord Gilstead was not making an assignation in his host's grounds. But then, what else could it be?

She did not want to disturb them and so she made her way further along the shrubbery before emerging close to the house. From there she proceeded to the library.

She felt a strange fluttering in her stomach as she opened the door, but whether it was from joy or fear she could not say. Her relationship with Lord

Amundel had been unusual, to say the least, and she had the feeling it was going to become more unusual still.

She went into the room. The sun was slanting in through the windows, making the heavy oak bookcases gleam. Flashes of light glanced off the golden lettering on the spines of the leather books, and dust motes danced in the sunbeams.

The scene was tranquil. But how tranquil would it remain once Lord Amundel arrived?

He was not long in coming. He was looking, if anything, more handsome than before. His dark hair was fashionably swept back from his face, accentuating the planes of his cheekbones and the firmness of his chin. His figure looked even more commanding than usual, as he was wearing pantaloons instead of the more usual breeches.

'Miss Morton.'

'Lord Amundel.'

He gave a wry smile.' That sounds very formal. Will you not call me Mark?'

'Certainly not,' she replied. To call him by his Christian name would introduce a further note of intimacy to an already far too intimate relationship.

'Very well. Lord Amundel it is. Thank you for coming,' he said formally.

She dropped him a mischievous curtsey. 'You're welcome, my lord.'

He laughed. 'What are we to do? If you insist on being formal, we must be formal. But I confess I would like to call you Catherine.' He had done so on occasion before, in the heat of the moment, but knew he must guard against further lapses - at least until she gave him permission to use her name.

'Perhaps in time,' she said.

He shook his head. 'This would be far easier if you did not have the most delightful dimple at the corner of your mouth,' he observed.

'Kindly keep your mind on the subject of our meeting. Which is . . . ?' she asked.

'Which is Miss Simpson's murder.' His manner became grave. He indicated a wing-back chair. 'Won't you sit down?'

She accepted, and sweeping her muslin skirt beneath her she arranged herself comfortably in the chair.

He sat opposite her, in a matching chair.

'Miss Simpson's death, I am convinced, was murder. Not just because your saddle's girth was cut through hours before a cord gave way on a heavy picture over her bed,' he said, Catherine having at last told him of the incident, 'but because of her mission here. You see, Miss Simpson was investigating another murder, the murder of her cousin two years ago.'

Catherine spoke gently. 'Forgive me, but that murder has already been solved. It was your brother who killed her.'

He shook his head. 'No. I do not say that because he was my brother,' he went on, seeing her expression, 'but because I believe it to be the truth.'

'But he said he couldn't live with the guilt —'

'And so he couldn't. But the guilt he could not live with was not the guilt of having caused her death, but the guilt of having been late for their meeting. They were lovers, as I expect you know, and were about to become engaged.'

'Oh, but I thought they were engaged?'

He shook his head. 'No. Although they would have been before the day was out. You see, my brother asked Miss Winter to meet him in the gardens in the evening so that he could propose. But, out riding that afternoon, his horse went lame and he was late returning to the house. He went down to the gardens as soon as he could but by that time it was too late. Miss Winter was already dead.'

'And if he had been there to meet her at the appointed time he felt she would have lived?'

'Yes.'

'Then - anyone could have killed her. Or, indeed, *her* death could have been an accident. It need not have been murder. It could have been a fall.'

'No. You see, a courting couple from the village had stolen into the grounds in order to take a short cut. As they were walking through the woodland they overheard snippets of conversation coming from the woodland, followed by the sound of a fall.'

Catherine looked at him searchingly. 'They were trustworthy, this courting couple?'

Lord Amundel nodded. 'Yes. They were thoroughly scrutinised. I have Lord Carlton's word for it that they were honest and reliable. Besides, they had no reason to lie.'

'And the conversation they overheard?'

He hesitated. 'That was what was so damning, and what led to the rumours about my brother. It was well known that he intended to propose to Miss Winter that evening, and the conversation the courting couple heard concerned the giving of a ring. "I've got something to show you," said a man's voice. Followed by a young woman's delighted cry of, "Oh, what a beautiful ring!" And then a startled cry, and then a thud. The courting couple went to see what had happened, and found Miss Winter dead at the bottom of the slope.'

'Even so it could have been an accident. She could have fallen, rather than being pushed.'

He shook his head. 'No. Her companion would then have either stayed with her or gone to raise the alarm. Instead he fled.'

'And the courting couple found her body.' Catherine frowned. 'I had thought it was Mr Glover who was the first person to find her,' said Catherine slowly.

'You're well informed,' said Lord Amundel. 'But no, he wasn't the first person to find her. He was, however, the first person from the house to find her - the courting couple left when they heard him arrive.'

'But if there was a house full of guests, in reality, anyone could have killed her,' said Catherine.

Lord Amundel nodded. 'Yes.'

Catherine looked at him, startled, and then everything fell into place. His interest in the murder; his searching of Miss Simpson's room; his concealment of his true identity - an identity that would have put the real murderer on guard. 'That's why you're here. You want to find out who the murderer was,' she said. Her voice was flat and unemotional. 'You're trying to clear your brother's name.'

He looked at her searchingly, as if deciding whether he could trust her, and then said simply,

'Yes.'

'Although you do realise, from what you have just told me, that the only person, on the face of it, with any reason to murder Miss Winter, is you?'

'I?' He was startled.

'You are the only person, as far as I know, who gained.'

'But how did I -?' he asked with a frown. And then his frown cleared. 'I gained a title. My brother was blamed for Miss Simpson's death. In grief and in guilt he killed himself. And I became the new Lord Amundel. And is that what you think happened?' he asked her seriously. 'Do you believe I am a murderer?'

She sensed that in some strange way her future hung in the balance, and that her answer to this question would affect her life for all time. Still, she searched her feelings and answered honestly: the one thing she had learnt most definitely from life was that she must always be true to herself. 'No, I don't.'

'Bless you for that,' he said. A light sparked in the depths of his velvety-brown eyes. 'For what it is worth, you are right. I didn't murder Miss Winter, nor did I covet my brother's title. And if I had wanted to kill him there would have been far easier ways of doing it. A group of footpads setting on him in London when I was far away; a jealous husband calling him out and shooting him - my brother was fond of women and was a terrible shot. These would have been far more certain ways of killing him, and no suspicion would have fallen on me. But I did not wish him dead.'

'Which leaves us with one question,' said

Catherine. 'Who killed Miss Winter?'

'Who indeed?'

'Well.' Catherine's manner became brisk. 'I think it is safe to assume that whoever killed Miss Winter also killed Miss Simpson?'

Lord Amundel nodded. 'It seems that the murderer realised Miss Simpson was not satisfied with her cousin's death and was trying to find out what really happened. And that was something the murderer could not allow.'

'Miss Simpson was looking for something,' agreed Catherine. 'And unfortunately anyone here could have know that.'

He looked at her enquiringly.

'Miss Simpson asked Lady Carlton if she might come to the Manor in order to look for an item belonging to her cousin that had gone missing. Lady Carlton was worried about it. She didn't think it was healthy. Nevertheless, she did not feel she could refuse.'

'And if Lady Carlton told you of her worries, she may well have told someone else.'

Catherine agreed. 'And even if she did not tell anyone else, they could easily have overheard our conversation.'

'And decided to take action before Miss Simpson found whatever it was she was looking for.'

They fell silent.

What *had* Miss Simpson been looking for? Catherine wondered. What could have been so important that the murderer could not afford for it to be found?

She expressed her thoughts to Lord Amundel.

'I don't know,' he admitted. 'Nor do I know why the murderer did not simply retrieve whatever it was themselves.'

'Unless Miss Simpson had already found it.'

'As you say. Unless she had already found it.'

The long case clock ticked in the corner.

Then he said, 'I think I might know what it was.'

Catherine was startled. 'You do?'

He paused, pursing his lips. The action pulled his tanned skin more tightly across his cheekbones. Catherine was seized with the urge to reach out and touch him.

'When I was in Miss Simpson's room I found —' He broke off, and then looked her in the eye. 'If we are to discover who the murderer is, I suggest we pool all our information.'

Catherine nodded. 'Agreed.'

'Very well. I found Miss Winter's journal.'

'Have you looked through it?'

'Briefly. It is full of the usual sort of thing - saucy remarks about teachers, romantic thoughts about young men . . .'

'But nothing important?'

'That is just the thing. In reading a young lady's journal - not something I'd wish to do in any other circumstances - I have no idea as to what is important. I have no knowledge of young lady's journals, you see.'

'And you think I might fare better with it?'

He nodded. 'I think you would be more likely to notice something unusual or out of place.'

'Do you have the journal with you?'

'It is in my room.'

Catherine was just about suggest they retire there - or, at least suggest that she accompany Lord Amundel to the end of the corridor - when the door opened and Miss Melissa Maltravers tripped in.

'Oh, Mr Stanton,' she said coyly, being unaware of his true identity. 'I had no idea you were here.'

'Miss Morton is also here,' he remarked wryly.

Melissa barely gave Catherine a look.

'But now I see you, may I ask you a great favour?'

'I am sure you will ask me, whether I give my permission or no,' he said dryly.

Melissa giggled. 'It's just that I do so want to learn how to waltz, and Mama says I am too young —' She paused appealingly, turning liquid blue eyes up to his.

'I would be happy to demonstrate,' he said, causing Melissa's eyes to sparkle. Then dashing her hopes by saying wryly, 'You may watch Miss Morton and I when we waltz at this evening's ball.'

Chapter Ten

'Oh, Miss Catherine, he didn't!' exclaimed Sally that evening, overcome with mirth.

Catherine's mouth twitched. 'Indeed he did!'

'Good for him. A perfect set-down. Saucy young thing!'

Catherine laughed. 'Miss Melissa was most put out.'

'Still, he'll have to face it: showing an eligible bachelor to a silly young girl's like waving a red rag in front of a bull. He's going to be inundated with attention at the ball.'

'If anyone can cope, Lord Amundel can.'

'And he'll have you to help him,' said Sally archly.

'Not you too, Sally,' Catherine sighed.

'You know my feelings, Miss Catherine. It's time you were married. But still, I can see you don't want to talk about it so I'll say no more. Now, you've decided on the white satin for the ball? The one with the overskirt of gold net?'

'Yes.'

'A good choice,' said Sally approvingly. 'You'll wear it with the diamonds?'

'No. I think something simple.'

'The gold necklet?'

'The very thing.'

'I'll see it's ready for you.'

Sally bustled out, leaving Catherine with an hour to fill before she needed to start to dress for the ball. She was glad that Lady Carlton had not cancelled it. Lady Carlton had at first considered doing so, but as a large number of neighbours had been invited it would not have been practical.

Catherine started to read her novel, but the sight of Miss Winter's journal, sitting innocently on her dressing-table, distracted her, until at last she could resist it no longer. She had been going to leave its perusal until after the ball, in fact until the following morning, when she would turn to it with a fresh mind, but her curiosity would not allow her any peace. Within those covers may lurk the identity of Miss Winter's murderer, and laying aside her novel, Catherine picked up the journal.

The journal covered the years from 1805 to the year 1814. Not every day was covered, in fact, far from it. To begin with, in particular, the entries were sporadic, dating from the time when Miss Winter was about eleven or twelve years old. The entries consisted of nothing more than a string of complaints, but nevertheless they gave Catherine an insight into Miss Winter's character, something she felt was important if she was to discover the truth about Miss Winter's murder. That character turned out to be ebullient.

Miss Travis is perfectly horrible - she makes me play the pianoforte until my fingers ache and will not seem to realise that I am no more musical than the housemaid's cat . . . Miss Fanshaw is a monster - she takes me out in all weathers, and speaks of fresh air and exercise in the reverent tone Father reserves for

111

his port . . . Miss Yeats is a coward - I have never heard such a caterwauling, and all because I put a frog in her desk . . .

Catherine smiled. Miss Winter had been a girl of spirit, it seemed! Which was perhaps why the murderer had adopted the ruse of giving her a ring, Catherine realised more thoughtfully. If Miss Winter had realised she was in danger she would have fought back, but if she was being given a present she would have been off her guard.

She leafed through the next few pages, where tutors and dancing masters came in for the same kind of comment.

Mr Letts is a dragon - can he not see I will never be able to dance the boulanger? . . . I cannot abide Mr Radcliffe - how he can make me take my painting out of doors in all this snow I do not know.

There were several more pages in similar vein. Catherine skimmed through them, wanting to find the more recent entries. She began to read more attentively when the subject matter changed. Miss Winter had evidently grown older, as the comments were no longer about childish exploits but were about the latest fashions, with whole pages being devoted to the descriptions of new or coveted items.

I have asked Father for an amber necklace . . . I would like to wear diamonds but Mother says I am far too young . . . . I have seen a most delightful shawl . . .

But whilst being interesting the pages gave no clue as to why Miss Winter had been murdered. Catherine skipped ahead, until the subject matter changed yet again. It now chiefly concerned young men.

Danced with Mr Jephet at Lady Turlington's . . .

Lord Trimble fetched me an ice . . . Went in to dinner with Mr Glover . . .

Catherine sat up. Went in to dinner with Mr Glover? Yes, they had known each other, of course. How else could Mr Glover have been besotted with Miss Winter?

Catherine read on. There were several more mentions of Mr Glover, and then mentions of Lord Amundel began to appear.

My Lord Amundel's brother, Catherine reminded herself - flushing a moment later as she realised that he was not *her* Lord Amundel at all.

And then the journal moved on. Balls and routs in London, followed by an invitation to the country - *to Lord and Lady Carlton's House, one Whitegates Manor . . .*

Without realising it, Catherine held her breath. There was an account of Miss Winter's arrival at the Manor, and some mention of other guests. *Lord and Lady Cuthbertson* - yes, Catherine had known they were there - *Lord and Lady Carlton*, of course - and *Lord Gilstead.*

Lord Gilstead. Yes. He, too, had been there.

She read on, more closely still. Miss Winter's arrangement to meet Lord Amundel, and her plans for the day of her death.

Am meeting   Jason just before dinner - if I don't miss my guess he has something special to ask ! ! ! ! ! Something special was heavily underlined. *Will meet him on my way back from the vicarage - need to look in on Mr Lucas . . .*

Mr Lucas.

Catherine sat back.

The Reverend Mr Lucas. She had forgotten all about Mr Lucas. But yes, she remembered him now. He had been at dinner on her first night at Whitegates Manor. So Miss Winter had gone to see Mr Lucas on the very evening of her murder.

Catherine felt a cold feeling invade the pit of her stomach. Mr Lucas. Miss Winter had gone to see Mr Lucas. So that Mr Lucas was the last person to have seen Miss Winter alive.

'It really is beautiful.' Sally stood back, admiring Catherine's ballgown.

It was a dazzling confection of white and gold. The white satin bodice, low yet decorously cut, was edged with the finest lace, whilst the white satin underskirt formed a beautiful backdrop to the overskirt of gold net. The net was as light as gossamer, floating airily over Catherine's delicate curves.

'And now your slippers,' said Sally, handing them to Catherine.

Catherine slid her feet into the white satin slippers, decorated with tiny gold rosettes, then viewed herself in the cheval glass. Her hair had been brushed until it shone, and was parted in the centre, with soft ringlets teased out to frame her face. Gold combs decorated with seed pearls held her hair in place.

She took out her simple gold necklet and passed the ends behind her neck to Sally, who fastened the clasp. Then she pulled on her gloves and picked up her painted fan and went downstairs.

The ball was not only for the guests who were staying at the Manor, but for the Carlton's friends and neighbours who lived round about as well. When

Catherine entered the ballroom there was already quite a throng. Mrs Maltravers was there with her daughters, besieging Sir George Osprey, a widower with three young children who was, in Mrs Maltravers' opinion, clearly in need of a wife.

The Thomas boys, far from being disconsolate, were amusing themselves by entertaining two pretty gentlemen farmer's daughters, who were there with their respectable parents.

Lady Cuthbertson was sitting in a corner giving as much trouble to Miss Rivers as possible, whilst Lord Cuthbertson sat beside her with a hesitant smile on his face.

Mr Glover and Mr Spence were in earnest conversation, and Lord Gilstead was smiling politely as Lady Carlton introduced him to an elderly, fierce-looking dowager.

And there was Lord Amundel. He was looking more handsome than any man had a right to look. The prevailing fashions suited him down to the ground, the superb cut of his tailcoat - really, he must go to the best tailor in London - showing the breadth of his shoulders and his tightly-fitting pantaloons revealing the lean firmness of his legs. Gleaming white linen accentuated the sun-bronze of his skin and a diamond tie-pin gleamed in his cravat.

He was talking to a small party of people Catherine did not know, friends of Lord and Lady Carlton's from the surrounding area, and she felt a sharp stab of something that felt suspiciously like jealousy as she realised he was laughing with the prettiest young woman in the room.

Fortunately at that moment Lord Carlton espied

her and she was absorbed with introductions of her own. She was introduced to Mr Trevelyan, a pleasant middle-aged gentleman who claimed her hand for the cotillion, and she was soon enjoying herself in the dance.

'I am glad to see the Thomas boys here,' remarked Mr Trevelyan as he led her from the floor once the dance was over. 'I knew Lady Carlton would like them.'

'You know them?' asked Catherine politely.

'Good Lord, yes. I've known the boys since they were children: Frederick, Edward and Tom. They stay with us regularly, and when Lady Carlton told me she was short of gentlemen for her party - it's a silly thing, but since the murder there are people who won't stay at Whitegates - I told her to invite them.' He was talking about Miss Winter's murder, Catherine realised - news of Miss Simpson's death had not been advertised, and even if he had heard of it he would have thought of it as an accident.

'Do they usually stay with you in the summer?' asked Catherine, suddenly alert.

'Every year,' said Mr Trevelyan pleasantly.

'And how far are you from Whitegates?' asked Catherine.

'Oh, no more than five miles or so. It's really no distance. No distance at all.'

So the Thomas boys had been in the area after all, two years before, when Miss Winter had been killed.

'Such a shame. Miss Winter was such a lovely girl. Frederick was quite sweet on her, you know. That is, until Amundel queered things for him. Oh, well, can't be helped. It's the way of the world, after all. Young girls like titles. And Amundel was a handsome young man by all accounts.'

'Miss Winter seems to have been very popular,' said Catherine.

'She was. A pretty young thing. Lively, too. Ah, well,' he sighed. 'It's a shame but there it is.'

Catherine's hand was soon claimed by Lord Gilstead, and after that by Lord Carlton.

'Is that Mr Lucas?' she asked innocently as Lord Carlton walked towards her in the steps of the dance.

Lord Carlton glanced to the side of the room, where the Reverend Mr Lucas was talking to a group of elderly ladies. They were nodding and shaking their heads by turn, and evidently agreeing with every word he said.

'Yes,' Lord Carlton replied.

'He seems to be a popular clergyman.'

'He is. Particularly with the old pussies!' said Lord Carlton with a twinkle in his eye.

As the steps of the dance took her closer to Mr Lucas and his admirers, Catherine overheard snippets of their conversation.

' . . . speak to her? She will not listen to me. I have told her off for having followers more times than I can count but it makes no difference . . . I have even quoted the bible to her but I cannot get her to mend her ways . . . '

'Never fear, dear lady. Leave it to me.'

'Oh, *thank* you, vicar.'

'Oh, my dear Reverend, what am I to do about my Molly . . . . ?'

Catherine smiled. It seemed the ladies were sure of a ready listener in Mr Lucas whenever they wanted to talk about their maidservants, and the problems the girls were causing them.

Could it have been a similar problem that had drawn Miss Winter to the Reverend Mr Lucas? Though young, Miss Winter would have had a maidservant. Had she wanted Mr Lucas's help to curb an impertinent girl? But as she wondered this, Catherine found herself recalling Miss Winter's journal. She could not believe that the irrepressible Miss Winter would have needed help to deal with a serving girl. And even if she had, surely she would have turned to her aunt?

What then? Had Miss Winter gone to make arrangements about her marriage? But at the time she was not even engaged. True, her journal showed that she anticipated the event, but even so, for a young lady to hint at her marriage before she was even engaged would be unthinkable. In fact, in this case it would have been unlikely as well as unthinkable, for Miss Winter was only holidaying at Whitegates Manor, and she would have wanted to make arrangements for her wedding at her own church, not at the Carltons' church. And of course she would not be the one making the arrangements anyway: that would have been taken care of by her family.

Catherine gave a sigh. She had no way of knowing why Miss Winter had visited Mr Lucas so she might as well stop guessing. Perhaps she would find out when she made a more careful reading of Miss Winter's journal.

'You are not tired, I hope?' asked Lord Carlton, hearing her sigh.

'No.' Catherine smiled. 'No, I am enjoying

myself.'

'That's the spirit!'

Catherine gave her full attention to Lord Carlton as the dance came to an end, and conversed with him politely as he escorted her back to the side of the room, where he left her in order to ask Mrs Maltravers to dance.

As the musicians tuned their instruments, Catherine saw Lord Amundel heading towards her.

'Miss Morton, I believe you owe me this dance.'

Catherine made him a curtsey and he took her hand, leading her back onto the floor, then turning her towards him he clasped her hand more firmly in his own and placed his other hand on her waist, just as the musicians played the opening notes of the waltz.

One, two, three; one, two, three . . . the rhythm was infectious, and Catherine found it taking her over as Lord Amundel swept her into the dance.

'And have you learnt anything useful from Miss Winter's journal?' he asked her, as he held her in his arms at the prescribed distance.

'Perhaps. But . . . would you think me callous if I said that I wanted to enjoy the rest of the evening, and leave all further thoughts of Miss Winter's death until tomorrow?'

'No. I would think you very sensible. Life is for the living, after all.'

He smiled down into her eyes, and drew her closer.

It felt so right that she wanted it to continue, but she knew it could not go on. 'You will create a scandal if you hold me so tightly,' she said. Her voice was trembling.

'We can't have that, can we?' he murmured.

119

They were approaching the French windows, and before she knew what was happening he had whirled her out onto the terrace, where he pressed her to him. If any of the biddies in the ballroom had seen they would have been scandalised indeed, but Catherine could only think how glorious it felt. Until all too soon they whirled in through the doors at the other end of the terrace and Lord Amundel put her gently away from him, holding her once more at the required distance.

'That,' he said softly, 'is how the waltz <u>should</u> be danced.'

The music came to an end. Regretfully, Catherine felt Lord Amundel's hand leave the small of her back and saw it drop to his   side.

'Miss Morton,' he said formally, bowing over her hand and kissing it; sending pleasurable ripples over her skin.

'Lord Amundel,' she said, dropping him a curtsey; before an elderly gentleman in a creaking corset claimed her hand.

The rest of the evening passed delightfully for Catherine. She was taken into supper by Lord Amundel, and afterwards she danced with him again. Twice was permissible; but to dance any more with the same man would have given rise to gossip, even at her advanced age, and so the second time was the last.

All too soon the ball was over; but Catherine contented herself with the fact that she would be seeing Lord Amundel in the morning. And then they would see if they could work out who the murderer was.

Chapter Eleven

Catherine woke early the following morning. The sun was up and the birds were singing, welcoming the new day. But despite the beautiful morning, Catherine was ill at ease. A new thought had occurred to her on waking. If Miss Simpson had come to Whitegates Manor because she was not satisfied with the conclusions drawn as to her cousin's murder, and if Miss Simpson had therefore been killed, then Lord Amundel, who had come to the Manor because he too was dissatisfied with the belief that his brother had killed Miss Winter, was also in danger.

She rang for Sally and, dressing hurriedly, went downstairs.

The house was quiet. Apart from the servants going about their daily tasks, no one else appeared to be up. Everyone was resting after the exertions of the ball and would in all likelihood not rise before twelve o'clock.

She was due to meet Lord Amundel in the library at ten o'clock, the time having been deliberately chosen so that they would stand a good chance of being uninterrupted, but Catherine had hoped that Lord Amundel might have been early. A glance at the clock, however, showed her that it was not yet half-past seven. It truly was early indeed!

How to pass the time until ten o'clock?

She glanced out of the window. The sky was clouding over and it looked like rain. She decided, therefore, not to venture outdoors, but to amuse herself by browsing amongst the books. She had finished her novel and wanted something new to read. Unfortunately, there were no Gothic novels on the shelves. However, she found a copy of *Robinson Crusoe* and, settling down on one of the window-seats, began to read.

She had not been reading for long when the door opened and closed again. She laid her book aside and was just about to reveal herself - for she was hidden by one of the bookcases - when the door opened again and an anxious voice asked, 'Did anyone see you?'

'No,' came Felicity Maltravers' voice.

Catherine hesitated. She had been going to reveal herself, but she was struck by the awkwardness of the situation. Felicity Maltravers was holding a secret assignation with Frederick Thomas, and the young lovers - for that is what their conversation revealed them to be - would hardly thank her for her interruption; and yet to remain where she was was perhaps even more awkward. Whilst she was trying to think of a way to reveal her presence in the least embarrassing manner possible, a turn in the conversation caught her attention.

'Did you tell him?' asked Mr Thomas.

Felicity's voice was hesitant. 'N . . . no.'

'You'll have to do it, Felicity.'

'But I can't. What if there's an innocent explanation?'

'An innocent explanation for Lord Gilstead going

into Miss Simpson's room whilst she was out riding?'

'Perhaps he had offered to lend her a book,' suggested Felicity nervously.

'No gentleman would go to an unmarried young lady's bedroom for any reason whatsoever, let alone go into it,' said Frederick.

'But it doesn't mean he was up to no good.'

'Felicity, I know you don't want to cause trouble, but Miss Simpson was killed by a falling picture. What if Lord Gilstead cut the cord?'

'I'm sure he didn't,; said Felicity unconvincingly.

'Felicity, you have to tell Lord Carlton. I will go with you. I will be with you every step of the way. But you have to tell him what you saw.'

'But what if Lord Gilstead is innocent?'

'Lord Carlton will be discreet. He's a man of the world, Felicity. He won't just leap in and accuse Lord Gilstead of murder, but he will know what to do.'

There was a silence, and Catherine could feel the tension in the room.

'Felicity, you have to tell him, and then it's out of your hands. You're too young to decide what to do in a case like this. You must be guided by me.'

'Oh, Frederick.'

'There, there, Charry,' he said affectionately. 'It'll be all right, I promise you. But you must tell Lord Carlton. It is his house, after all. He has a right to know.'

There came a long sigh. 'I suppose you are right.'

'You know I am. Come, let's get it over with.'

'But Lord Carlton won't be up yet.'

'He's in the stables. I went to check on my horse, and he was already there. It will take more than a ball

---

to keep Lord Carlton in bed on a summer morning.'

Felicity evidently allowed herself to be persuaded, because the door opened and closed again.

Leaving Catherine with much food for thought.

Lord Amundel entered the library at a quarter to ten.

'You're here,' he said, his voice a mixture of surprise and pleasure.

'I have been here since half-past seven,' she admitted.

'You couldn't sleep?'

'No.'

'Because of something you read in Miss Winter's journal?'

'Not exactly, no.'

'But you did discover something?'

'A number of things, yes. But before I tell you about them I want you to promise me you will leave here. Go right away.'

His eyebrows raised in surprise. Then he frowned. 'Have I done something to offend you?' he asked.

'No.' She was startled. Then, seeing how her comments must have sounded she gave a rueful smile. 'I did not mean that I wanted you to leave for my sake. I meant I wanted you to leave for your own.' She explained to him that she thought his life was in danger, and why.

He was thoughtful. 'And would it matter to you, if something happened to me.'

She nodded. 'Yes. It would.'

He smiled at her; a warm smile. 'Still, I think it better if I stay. I am not an easy target. I spent a number of years in the army, remember. I know how to look after myself.'

She shook her head. 'No. I don't accept that. Miss Winter was attacked openly because she was weak but with you it will be different. You are a man.'

'As I mean to prove to you . . . when you are ready,' he said.

There was a sudden charge in the atmosphere, and Catherine shivered from head to foot.

'That is not what I meant.' She deliberately avoided making any further comment on his remark; she did not trust herself to speak of it. 'I meant that the murderer may attack you less openly. With poison, perhaps - something you will have no defence against.'

He considered. 'It is possible,' he said.

'Then you will go?'

'No.'

'But . . . '

'I cannot find out who killed Miss Winter if I go, and I must discover it. I owe it to my brother.'

She nodded. She wished he would leave, go right away from danger, but she recognised that he could not do it.

'So. Will you tell me what you have discovered?'

Catherine settled herself into the window seat, and revealed that Miss Winter had had an appointment with the vicar on the day of her murder.

'So Lucas was the last one - apart from the murderer - to see her alive.'

'Yes.'

'But why should the Reverend Mr Lucas wish to kill her?'

'As to that, who can say? But some possibilities

have occurred to me. Mr Lucas has a great following among the elderly ladies roundabout. He helps them out when they have problems with their serving girls. If the girls won't accept that they are to have no life of their own, but are expected to devote themselves to their mistresses and dispense with followers forthwith, then the Reverend Mr Lucas has a word with them. What if Miss Winter had discovered him with a serving maid herself?'

His eyes danced. 'I see you have an active imagination!'

'That is just the trouble,' said Catherine. 'Since Miss Simpson's murder, I have imagined the most terrible things about almost everybody, casting them all in the light of a murderer. Mr Glover is a suspect because he was enamoured of both the dead girls; Mrs Maltravers is a suspect because she wanted her daughter to marry your brother - ah! I see that is news to you. And Clarissa Maltravers is a suspect because she wanted to marry your brother. Then there is Mr Spence. He thinks the murder will make him an object of interest, and therefore help him to find a backer for his plays. And as if that isn't enough, Mr Frederick Thomas was supposedly in love with Miss Winter, and could have killed her in a fit of jealous rage when he realised she was about to marry your brother.'

She hesitated.

'Yes?'

'And then there is a conversation I overheard whilst waiting for you here in the library . . .'

Briefly she told him what she had overheard. He became restless, and strode across the room and back.

'This about Gilstead. I don't like to say it - he was

a good officer and fought well in the war - but there were rumours about him. Apparently one of the camp followers fell down a deep ravine. Gilstead was the last one to have been with her.'

'And he seems such a pleasant man,' said Catherine.

'He may well *be* a pleasant man: rumours are not the same as facts. Even so, I am glad that Frederick managed to persuade Felicity to confide in Lord Carlton.'

Catherine looked anxious.

'What is it?' he asked.

'Nothing.'

'There is something. Won't you tell me what it is?'

'It's nothing. As I said, I have become very suspicious over the last few days.'

'And?'

'And . . . Lord Carlton changed the cord on the picture very quickly. What if he did so for a reason?'

'You *have* become suspicious,' said Lord Amundel.

'That is the worst of a situation like this.'

He nodded. 'Perhaps it is for the best. But I doubt if Lord Carlton had anything to do with it. Committing a murder on his own property would hardly be the wisest thing to do.'

Catherine was reassured. She did not want to suspect Lord Carton of anything so heinous, and was glad Lord Amundel found it unlikely.

'The trouble is,' she said, 'that almost anyone *could* have done it. What we need is evidence of who actually *did* do it. We need some kind of proof.'

'Which is just what we are unlikely to find. No, we

must continue as we are.' He was thoughtful. 'Maybe Gilstead is not the only one with something unfortunate in his past. Maybe some of the other guests have been connected with suspicious circumstances.'

Catherine nodded slowly, her thoughts travelling down new channels. 'Lord Cuthbertson's young half-brother drowned. Is it possible that the boy's death was not an accident, and that Lord Cuthbertson drowned him?'

'For what reason?' Lord Amundel asked.

'Perhaps Lord Cuthbertson's father left the child a substantial sum of money which reverted to Lord Cuthbertson on the child's death.'

'And why would that lead him to murder Miss Winter?'

'Perhaps,' said Catherine, 'because she saw what he did.'

'It's possible,' he agreed. 'Is there any way we can find out if Lord Cuthbertson was alone with the boy when he drowned? And if Miss Winter was at the house at the time?'

'I'll ask Miss Rivers. She is a fountain of information where the Cuthbertsons are concerned.'

'Good. And I think I will pay the Reverend Mr Lucas a visit. I would like to know why Miss Winter went to see him on the day she was murdered.'

'Oh, my dear, it was a terrible tragedy.' Miss Rivers, who was embroidering a petticoat, was enjoying having someone to talk to. 'Quite, quite dreadful.'

'It must have been,' said Catherine sympathetically.

'Lord Cuthbertson took it hard. Very hard. And so did Lady Cuthbertson, of course.'

'The boy drowned, I think you said?'

'Yes. That's right. He was playing on the boats. Such a high-spirited child. Jumping from one to the other. The rowing boats,' she explained to Catherine. 'They were all tied up at the jetty. There was to be a boating party, you see, later that day. On the lake. Moorfield is a beautiful estate. The lake is a large one, and Lord Cuthbertson often held boating parties for one or two select friends. But he does not hold them any more.'

'And Lord Cuthbertson had taken his brother down to see the boats?' asked Catherine, trying to focus Miss Rivers' attention.

'Not to see the boats, no. Just to check on things in general.'

'It must have been a great shock for him.'

Miss Rivers shook her head sympathetically. 'It was a great shock for them all. Lord Cuthbertson, Lady Cuthbertson, Sir William - Sir William Carlisle, the Cuthbertsons' neighbour, and the local magistrate, you know. And of course the servants. They were all deeply shocked.'

'Ah! Then he was not alone with the boy,' she said.

'Oh, no. Dear me, no. That was what made it so awful. There were so many people there. But they could only look on in horror. You see, none of them could swim.'

Catherine sighed. It seemed she was getting nowhere. Still, she ought to finish checking out this theory. 'The boy was well provided for?' she asked.

'Oh, yes. Lord Cuthbertson had made the boy his heir.'

'Lord Cuthbertson's father, then, did not provide for the boy?'

'No. He left that to Lord Cuthbertson.'

Catherine gave an inward sigh. So Lord Cuthbertson had not gained by the boy's death. On top of which the accident had taken place in front of the local magistrate and a group of servants.

And as if to underline the fact that Lord Cuthbertson, therefore, would have had no reason to kill Miss Winter, a further perusal of Miss Winter's journal showed that at the time of the little boy's death Miss Winter, far from witnessing it, had been at the other end of the country enjoying her London Season.

Catherine sighed. The situation, instead of becoming clearer, was becoming more puzzling.

Her gaze wandered to the window. The day was, for the moment, fine, and she wondered whether she should take a walk. But seeing Mr Glover practising his archery she had a better idea. He had been the first person from the house to reach Miss Winter. Perhaps he could tell her more about the incident.

Chapter Twelve

'Mr Glover. How pleased I am to see you. I have often wanted to have a go at archery, but I have never had the opportunity. I wonder if you would show me what to do?'

Mr Glover looked at her morosely. Catherine, however, was not put off.

'It doesn't seem right,' he said. 'Carrying on as if nothing had happened. Miss Simpson was an angel and now she's dead. That damned picture! Carlton should be shot.' He remembered that he was speaking to a lady and mumbled an apology. 'But he should have made sure the damn - dashed thing was safe,' he said belligerently.

'It was a terrible thing to happen,' said Catherine, 'but I don't believe Lord Carlton can be blamed. I am sure he is as upset as everyone else about the accident.'

'Hah!' Mr Glover's exclamation was bitter.

'I think you cannot blame the rest of the guests for carrying on as though nothing has happened,' said Catherine gently. 'After all, Miss Simpson was not well known to anyone here - although I believe you knew her well.'

He shifted uncomfortably and fiddled with the string of his bow. 'I wouldn't say that.'

'I beg your pardon.' Catherine had noticed his discomfort but felt it better not to press the point for the moment. 'I thought you had known her before. But perhaps it is her cousin, Miss Winter, I am thinking of.'

'When I think of her . . . ' he broke out explosively. Then, morosely, 'This place is cursed.'

'It must have been hard for you. I believe you found Miss Winter's body,' said Catherine.

He gripped the bow more tightly. 'If only I had been a minute sooner.'

'It is fortunate you were nearby at the time.'

'Fortunate! If only I had not been —' He stopped abruptly.

'Yes?' Catherine pushed him gently.

He appeared to wrestle with himself and then growled, 'Nothing.' A minute later he said, 'I think you wanted me to show you how to shoot?'

'If it would not be too much trouble.'

'No. Of course not.'

He made a visible effort to control himself and then said to Catherine, 'First you must learn how to use the bow. Here, hold it like this.'

He demonstrated, and Catherine took up her bow. It was lighter than she had expected, but unwieldy.

'Now. Practise pulling back on the string.'

Catherine tried to do as he said, following his instructions, but she found it difficult.

'Here.'

He put his arms round her to help her and added his strength to hers.

She thought obliquely of Lord Amundel's touch. If he had put his arms around her she would have felt weak, but when Mr Glover did so she felt perfectly normal.

After a few minutes she was able to pull back the bow herself, letting it go when Mr Glover directed her to. She practised the movement a number of times on her own until she felt comfortable with it, and then Mr Glover showed her how to fit an arrow. She bent the bow and let the arrow fly. It went wide of the target, landing in the grass beyond.

'Never mind. Try again,' he said.

The lesson lasted for half an hour. But no matter how many times Catherine tried to re-introduce the subject of Miss Winter's death, Mr Glover would not join in. Whatever he had been going to say was lost, and Catherine could only hope that it hadn't been important.

'Did you discover why Miss Winter went to see Mr Lucas?' asked Catherine later that day as she strolled through the orchard with Lord Amundel.

'No. He denied all knowledge of a meeting, and declared that Miss Winter had not called on him at any time during her stay here.'

'Was he telling the truth, do you think?'

'It's hard to be sure. He could have been. But equally, he could have been hiding something.'

'I think,' said Catherine slowly, 'that if he'd been hiding something he'd have admitted to the visit but lied about its reason. That way he would have seemed above reproach.'

'Whereas this way he leaves himself open to doubts about his honesty? It may be so.'

'In that case, was Miss Winter prevented from

going to see him, or did she merely change her mind?'

Lord Amundel offered her his arm. 'That is something I suspect we will never know. However, I did learn something useful. The courting couple from the village were not in fact a courting couple from the village. They were a village girl and Lord Gilstead.'

'Lord Gilstead?'

'Yes.'

Catherine let out a long breath. 'He seems such a quiet man, but I keep coming upon evidence that he is not what he seems. First, Felicity saw him going into Miss Simpson's room, then you tell me that there were rumours about him in the army, and now - now he was with one of the girls from the village. What could he have possibly been doing - oh. Oh, how stupid of me. Of course.' She paused for a minute, annoyed with herself for having been so obtuse. Then she said, 'Is his testimony reliable, do you think?'

Lord Amundel nodded. 'I think so. Yes. Gilstead's an honourable man. I don't think he would have lied about such a serious matter. Besides, the young woman agreed with his account.'

'But could have been paid to do so,' Catherine pointed out.

'That is possible.'

'How did you find out?' asked Catherine.

'It was Lucas. He let it slip when the conversation turned to Miss Winter's death. As I had been in the army with Gilstead, and was now staying at the same house with him, Mr Lucas assumed that Gilstead and I are close friends. As such, he thought I already knew it was Gilstead who had overheard the conversation. I did not disabuse him of the notion.'

'And did he say why Lord Gilstead's rôle was not made public?'

'No. But given the circumstances I would expect it was to protect the identity of the young woman. She, too, was never named. Lord Carlton is the local magistrate and he enquired into the matter most fully, but having done so I imagine he saw no need to embarrass a young girl from the village and one of his guests. Referring to them simply as "a courting couple" protected their identities.'

'Was it Lord Carlton you asked about Miss Winter's murder? To begin with? When you first wanted to clear your brother's name?' asked Catherine.

'Yes. He told me that a courting couple from the village had overheard Miss Winter's conversation, and that the conversation had centred round a ring.'

'And that was what started the rumours that your brother had killed Miss Winters.'

'Yes.'

'He was never prosecuted?' she saw his mouth tighten. 'Forgive me, I should not have asked.'

He appeared to consider. Then he answered the question. 'No. There was no evidence against him. But rumour spread, and when he killed himself his suicide was taken as confirmation of his guilt.'

They walked on in silence. Despite the darkness of their conversation, Catherine felt entirely at ease. She had never felt so at ease with anyone as she felt with Lord Amundel, and she reflected on the strangeness of the fact that a man who could so move her so strongly could also make her feel entirely calm.

'And you?' he asked at last. 'Did you discover

anything of interest in your own enquiries?'

'Very little. Lord Cuthbertson's half-brother drowned in full view of the local magistrate, as well as Lady Cuthbertson and a group of servants.'

'Then there is nothing there.'

'But Mr Glover - I am not sure about Mr Glover. He seemed very uncomfortable. He also seemed to be on the verge of telling me something important. But it could be nothing. He is upset over Miss Simpson's death, and he feels that to continue with the house party is callous in light of it. That could be the cause of his abrasiveness.'

'And yet he stays,' remarked Lord Amundel.

'Yes,' said Catherine thoughtfully. 'He stays.'

Lord Amundel was silent for a minute. Then he said, 'I think it is time we found out who has an alibi for the first murder. For the second, as the cord could have been cut at any time, it will be impossible to rule anyone out. I have already had my man questioning the servants - discreetly, of course - but they did not see anyone entering or leaving Miss Simpson's room, or hanging about in the corridor. So we have to assume that any one of the guests could have done it. But with Miss Winter's death we have a clear time. It should be possible to find out who was where; also who was alone and who was in company.'

'It will be difficult. Two years have gone by.'

'It will. Nevertheless, it must be attempted.'

Catherine agreed, and Lord Amundel undertook to check on the movements of those who had not been staying at the Manor. As he knew some of the families in the neighbourhood it would be easy for him to ride over to see them and pay his respects, and then turn the conversation to the evening of Miss Winter's death.

'Let us hope it sheds some light on the matter,' he said.

Catherine heartily agreed.

Afternoon tea was being served when Catherine returned to the house. Lord Amundel had left her to go and see his groom, and she went into the drawing-room alone. There in the corner was Miss Rivers, talking to Lady Carlton, who was listening with great forbearance.

' . . . and not an ounce of vanity in her,' Miss Rivers was saying. 'Lord Cuthbertson had her portrait painted and hung it in the hall, but Lady Cuthbertson was not having any of it. "Put it in the attic, Emmy," she said to me, and that is where it hangs to this day. Though I am sure we . . . '

'And a good thing too.' Clarissa Maltravers, on the other side of the room, giggled behind her fan. 'A face like that could sour the milk!'

Melissa joined in the muffled laughter, but Felicity did not: Felicity, Catherine noticed, was nowhere to be seen. Did she go and see Lord Carlton? wondered Catherine. And if so, what was the result of her encounter with him?

There were only two people who could give her the answer to that question and if Felicity was nowhere to be seen, then Lord Carlton was. Plucking up her courage Catherine went over to him and engaged him in conversation.

'I understand Felicity Maltravers came to see you this morning,' she said when she was comfortably settled with a cup of tea.

Lord Carlton looked at her shrewdly. 'Now what makes you say that, I wonder?'

Catherine gave a rueful smile. 'I must confess. I overheard her conversation this morning and wondered what you made of the fact that Lord Gilstead was in Miss Simpson's room.'

'Did you indeed.' Lord Carlton was thoughtful.

'Are you not going to enlighten me?' she asked.

'If I thought it was ghoulish curiosity . . . But I know you too well for that. Very well. Felicity Maltravers did come and see me this morning. And yes, she did tell me that she saw Lord Gilstead coming out of Miss Simpson's room whilst Miss Simpson was out riding.'

Not out riding, thought Catherine, merely in the stables. But did not say so. Aloud she said, 'And do you believe her?'

He looked thoughtful. 'Yes,' he said at last. 'I do. The Maltravers' girls might be silly and flighty but they are not prone to making things up. I believe her.'

'And does it not strike you as strange?'

He nodded. 'Yes. It does.'

'Have you asked him about it?'

'I have.'

'And?'

'And what he told me was in the strictest confidence.'

Catherine put down her cup. 'Forgive me for speaking plainly, but Miss Simpson is dead. Has it not occurred to you that Lord Gilstead might have had something to do with that death?'

'By cutting the cord on the picture?' Lord Carlton

asked.

Catherine was startled.

'You are not the only one in the house with a mind, Catherine,' he said. 'Yes, it has occurred to me. But you see, I examined the cord on the picture before I had it replaced. It had not been cut.'

'It had frayed?'

'Yes.'

'And was the fraying natural, or had someone perhaps rubbed it over the nail on which it hung, fraying it on purpose?'

'It is impossible to say.'

Catherine frowned. 'I see.'

'Yes. I believe you do. We have no way of knowing whether Miss Simpson's death was an accident, or murder.'

Catherine looked at him in sudden apprehension. She had not realised where their conversation was taking them, but now that it had reached this point she was suddenly aware of how foolish she had been. If Lord Carlton was the murderer she had let him know that she was suspicious.

'And no, Catherine,' said Lord Carlton gently, 'I did not kill her.'

'Oh, but I never thought —'

'Oh, but you did. Fortunately for you I am not a murderer. But let me give you a word of advice. If you wonder about Miss Simpson's death, wonder in private. To do anything else may not be safe.'

And with these cryptic words he left her side and went to join Mr Frederick Thomas, who had just entered the room.

Catherine's head was spinning when she returned to her room that night.

'You look tired,' said Sally.

'I am.' Catherine sat on the edge of the bed and kicked off her satin slippers. 'I'm exhausted.'

'It's all this thinking about Miss Simpson's death.'

'Do you know, Sally, it seems that almost everyone here had a motive for murdering Miss Simpson. And everyone had the opportunity.'

'In that case, I should let it rest. It's not your responsibility, after all.'

Catherine sighed. 'Perhaps you are right.'

'Why don't I fix you a nice bath?' suggested Sally.

'A nice bath. Yes, that would be the very thing.'

'And afterwards an early night. And no,' Sally said, her eyes following Catherine's to Miss Winter's journal, which lay on the bedside table. 'No reading of that, either, tonight.'

Catherine felt a tug towards the journal, which she had skimmed through already but had not yet read carefully. She fought against it. Sally was right. She would be better off forgetting about the whole thing,

'I'll read my novel instead.'

'That's the idea,' said Sally approvingly.

Sally bustled out of the room and returned not long afterwards with a train of maids, all carrying jugs of hot water. Clouds of steam emanated from Catherine's dressing-room, and by the time Catherine entered it the hip bath was already half full. She slipped out of her clothes and into the soothing hot water.

This is heavenly, thought Catherine as she lay back in the water. She felt her shoulders loosen and realised that she had been very tense. All this inquisitiveness was not good for her. She would give it up forthwith.

Growing more and more relaxed by the minute she felt herself growing sleepy and at last stirred herself, washing and then climbing out of the bath, before pulling on her night-gown and climbing into bed.

Sally had moved Miss Winter's journal, she noticed, putting it on the window-seat. She was glad. She would not be tempted to read it if she had to get out of bed to fetch it. Instead she turned to *Robinson Crusoe*, and read until she was almost asleep. Then, blowing out the candle she lay down and was asleep as soon as her head touched the pillow.

True to her determination to let Miss Simpson's death rest, Catherine decided to go down to the village the following morning. The walk would do her good, she felt, and besides, it would be nice to get away from Whitegates, even if it was only for a short while.

Dressed in a walking gown of spotted sarsenet she felt pleasantly cool. Fortunately the dress had no train - the fashions in previous years had been so impractical! - but it was still decidedly elegant, being decorated round the hem with a row of pleated frills. With her bonnet on her head and her parasol in her hand she felt she was prepared for every eventuality.

She had not gone halfway to the gate, however, when she heard a 'Cooee!' behind her.

She sighed at the sound, but nevertheless turned round politely and waited for Miss Dunstan to join her.

'Are you going into the village? What fun! We can go together, and have a comfortable cose on the way.'

Catherine resigned herself to Miss Dunstan's

company and together the two ladies continued their walk. It was not that she disliked Miss Dunstan, it was simply being in company with someone so relentlessly cheerful had a tendency to make her want to groan. So far she had seen little of the middle-aged spinster, but she realised that was about to change.

'Is this not a marvellous thing, the marriage of our dear Princess Charlotte to Prince Leopold? Such a fairy-tale romance. Only think, she turned down the man her father had chosen for her because of her love for the Prince. It is like something out of a story-book, is it not? And of course they are to live at Claremont Park,' she went on, without giving Catherine time to reply. 'As well as in London, of course. Just think, they are to have an income of sixty thousand pounds a year. Sixty thousand! What I could not do with sixty thousand pounds! I would buy a whole new set of caps for Mother, and Donner and Blitzen would have a golden collar each! And yet they are neither of them extravagant, in fact they are almost staid,' she said, moving blithely from her dogs to Princess Charlotte and Prince Leopold in half a breath, without realising the strange image her words were conjuring up. 'Ah! What marriage does for a woman.'

She sighed. But a second later she was off again. 'Do you know, the Princess is so patriotic that she will not wear a foreign gown? She has all of hers made in London. Fancy that! Oh, it will be so wonderful when she is on the throne. Not that I have anything against the Regent,' she added hastily. 'I am sure he is a fine man. But just the teeniest bit reckless. Take the Pavilion at Brighton. Have you seen it, Miss Morton?'

'I —' Catherine began.

'It is like a Nabob's palace,' went on Miss Dunstan. 'Though why I say that I am sure I don't know, for I have never seen a Nabob's palace in my life. And, truth to tell, I have no very clear idea of what a Nabob is. Still, I am sure it is just like it. Do you know, I went inside when I was younger? You've never seen the like. Everything came from China, or at the very least it pretended to be Chinese. There were lanterns and dragons - not real ones, of course! Though real ones might have been rather fun! - and lotus leaves and serpents and pagodas and goodness knows what else. It was splendid, of course, quite splendid, but do you know, Miss Morton, I was afraid to move? There were so many ornaments and vases and such that it was like being in a shop, and I was frightened that if I knocked something over accidentally the Regent would ask me to pay for it! Though I am sure he would never have dreamt of doing anything so vulgar. But, still, I was glad to get back home. And now dear Princess Charlotte is married and, with luck, will be expecting any time soon. And then we will have a dear little baby and someone new to sit upon the throne. It will be . . . '

Her conversation rattled on, and Catherine was free to let her thoughts wander as they would. Miss Dunstan did not require someone to talk to, but rather to talk at. It would have irritated Catherine in another person, but knowing that Miss Dunstan led a dull life looking after her mother and that she was rarely in company, so that she rarely had any opportunity for conversation, Catherine was happy to provide Miss Dunstan with an outlet for her volubility.

They came at last to the village, and Miss Dunstan

excused herself, saying she had some errands to run for her mother, leaving Catherine to look round at her leisure.

The village was small but had a number of interesting shops. There was an intriguing-looking milliner's, and it was towards this that Catherine turned her steps.

The next half hour was spent in delightful contemplation of a number of bonnets and hats. Tall crowns were fashionable, and Catherine examined half a dozen bonnets with crowns quite ten inches high. Some were trimmed with ribbon, some with artificial flowers, and one was adorned with white ostrich plumes that curled fetchingly from the top of the crown to the bottom.

She should not really indulge herself, as she had quite enough bonnets, but the temptation was too much for her and she told a very pleased milliner she would take it.

As the milliner placed it in a hat box, Catherine's glance travelled idly round the shop and across the models in the window. As it did so she saw a woman walking by whom she thought she recognised. But where had she seen her before?

'Is anything wrong?' asked the milliner, seeing Catherine frown.

'No. It's nothing. It's just that I can't help thinking I've seen that person before.'

The milliner followed Catherine's gaze. 'That's Mary Miller. She lives in the village. She's old Ben Miller's daughter.'

'Ah,' said Catherine, unenlightened.

'Such a comfort to him, is Mary,' went on the

milliner, tying the box with a ribbon. 'Especially after Susan. Going off to the continent like that, following the drum. But there, least said, soonest mended. Of course, what with their mother being a fallen woman,' went on the milliner, blithely ignoring her own dictum, 'it's not surprising really. Susan was always wild. Always one for the regiments. It takes some girls like that. It's the red coats. Mary was all for going after her, but old Ben wouldn't let her. And quite right too. One daughter running after soldiers is bad enough without the other one following - even if the other one's only going looking for the first. "She's no daughter of mine," said Ben. "And don't you have anything to do with her either, Mary, or I'll cut you off as well". Hard, but fair. You can't be too careful with girls. Now there's your bonnet, Miss, and if you change your mind about the French hat you've only to ask. If the shop's not open a knock will always bring me to the door.'

She handed Catherine the box, and thanking her Catherine left the shop.

Following the drum. As soon as the milliner had said it Catherine remembered where she had seen the young woman before: talking to Lord Gilstead in the shrubbery.

Was Susan the young woman Lord Amundel had mentioned in connection with Lord Gilstead, Catherine wondered? It was possible.

But she was not meant to be thinking suspiciously about her fellow guests, she reminded herself. She had done with all that. Lord Gilstead's assignations were his own affair. They were no business of hers.

She spent a further hour in the village, looking in

at the haberdasher's and the modiste's, and then, her thoughts firmly fixed on trivialities, she returned to the Manor.

A day spent in idle recreation had done Catherine good. As well as walking into the village in the morning she had been rowed across the lake by the youngest Mr Thomas in the afternoon, in company with Mr Spence and Melissa Maltravers. She had put aside all her suspicions and had joined in the conversation on the latest plays with gusto. It was with a much quieter mind that she finally went to bed.

Miss Winter's journal was not only out of reach, it was now put away out of sight in a drawer, and already Catherine felt its pull fading. She picked up *Robinson Crusoe* and began to read. How delightful it was for him to find Friday, and to have a companion at last.

Then, blowing out the candle she settled down for the night.

Only to find herself sitting bolt upright in the early hours of the following morning, all her good intentions forgotten; for her dreams, as well as being turbulent, had been full of meaning. They had pointed her to something so overwhelmingly important that she could not ignore it: the very piece of evidence she had been missing.

'So that's what Miss Simpson was looking for,' she said.

Chapter Thirteen

'What time is it?' asked Catherine the following morning, waking to find her room flooded in daylight.

'Ten o'clock,' said Sally, whose entrance had woken Catherine.

'Ten o'clock!' Catherine threw back the covers and leapt out of bed.

'What ever is the matter?' asked Sally in surprise.

'I know what she was looking for,' Catherine said cryptically.

'Who?' asked Sally, bemused.

'Miss Simpson.'

'I thought you'd finished with all that,' said Sally, not taking any trouble to hide her displeasure.

'I had. But then it came to me. What Miss Simpson was looking for. Which means it will either be in her room with her effects, or it will be where it's always been. It's the answer, Sally. The answer to the riddle. The piece of evidence I knew we would need if we were ever to find out who killed Miss Winter and Miss Simpson.'

'We?' asked Sally.

Catherine flushed. She had not meant to give herself away, but in her excitement she had not been as guarded as she should have been.

'Yes, we,' she said as coolly as she could. 'Lord

Amundel has been as anxious as I to find out who killed Miss Winter and her cousin.'

'Well, if you're determined, there's nothing I can do to stop you. But if you really think you're on the track of the murderer then take care. If you're right, then someone in this house has killed twice already. They won't draw the line at doing it again.'

Catherine hesitated. Sally was right. This wasn't a game.

She went over to the writing-table and scribbled a note, throwing down the quill as soon as she had finished. 'If for any reason I don't come back, give this note to Lord Amundel. It tells him where I am going and why.'

Sally looked at the note curiously.

'No, Sally, I'm not going to tell you what's in it. The least said the better - for now.'

Sally frowned. 'I don't like it. Why not tell Lord Amundel and take him with you?'

'I intend to,' said Catherine. 'The note is just in case of emergencies.'

'Don't go doing anything dangerous.'

'I won't.'

Then, having washed and dressed whilst she was talking, Catherine headed towards the door.

'What about your breakfast?' Sally asked.

'I haven't time for breakfast.' Seeing Sally's face she went over to the tray which the maid had brought in and took a few sips of chocolate and a bite of hot roll. It tasted good. She was eager to be on her way, but the food was tempting and besides, she knew she would be more alert if she ate. So sitting down she finished the breakfast Sally had brought for her and then she was on her way.

Miss Simpson's room did not reveal what she was looking for. It seemed, then that Miss Simpson had not found it. Which meant that, unless it had been reclaimed by the murderer, it was where it had been all this time . .

Catherine went out into the gardens and took the route she had taken on her first day at Whitegates Manor. She crossed the lawns, passed the rose gardens and then made her way to the woodland.

It was cool beneath the trees. For a minute she wished she had stopped to put on her pelisse. But another layer of clothing would only have made her task more difficult.

Not for the first time she wished that women were allowed to wear bifurcated garments. As a child she had borrowed her father's breeches on occasion - strictly without his knowledge! - and found them most convenient for climbing trees or - horror of horrors! - riding astride. But as she had got older such pranks had had to cease, and now she was forced to scramble down the slope where Miss Winter had been killed hampered by her skirts. However, she managed it, and then stood looking up the hill to the point from which Miss Winter had fallen.

Now, what led up to Miss Winter's fall? she asked herself, remembering everything she had been told about the incident. Miss Winter had been in the woodland, and, on Lord Gilstead's evidence - if that was to be trusted - not alone. The man she had been with had said, "I've got something to show you!" and she had replied, "Oh! What a beautiful ring!"

Catherine pictured the scene: a gentleman giving a young lady a ring; her taking it; being distracted by the beauty of the ring; not seeing the danger she was in; being pushed; falling down, down, down - still clutching the ring, but somewhere along the way letting go . . . . Yes, she must have let it go, because if not it would have been amongst her effects. And it had not been, of that Catherine was sure, because she was now convinced that that was what Miss Simpson had been searching for. Not her cousin's journal, which Catherine suspected she had had all along, but the ring. So where was it? That was the notion that had woken Catherine in the middle of the night. The ring must be somewhere, and Catherine guessed that Miss Winter must have dropped it as she had fallen. Otherwise, if she had been wearing it or still clutching it when she was found, it would have been returned with the rest of her effects. So unless the murderer had picked it up again it must still be in the woodland.

But surely the murderer would have picked it up? thought Catherine, suddenly doubting herself.

Yes, if he had had time. But he had not had time. He had had to leave the scene immediately so that he would not be discovered: it had taken Mr Glover only a minute to reach Miss Winter and by that time the murderer had fled. And afterwards the murderer would have found it difficult to return to the spot without attracting attention, particularly as the house party had broken up soon afterwards and he would have had to leave. He could have returned at night, perhaps, but in the dark, with a large area of woodland to search, his chances of recovering it would have been slim.

When had Miss Simpson realised that there had

been no strange ring amongst her cousin's effects? Catherine wondered. Probably not for a while. But when she had done she had been curious. Where was it? And had it come from the man who was about to become her fiancé, or from someone else?

This was the thought that had driven Miss Simpson, Catherine felt convinced. Where was the ring? And, once found, who did it belong to?

Catherine's eyes raked the slope. Trees and rhododendrons grew at intervals all the way down. Roots poked out at odd angles from the earth, and rotting leaves lay in drifts, in places three or four inches deep. It would take hours to search, perhaps days.

The thought was daunting. Still, she had to try.

Several hours later, she was beginning to think it was a lost cause. Her search had had to be broken off a number of times as various guests had passed close by, and she realised how difficult it must have been for the murderer if he had tried to find it. Even so, she had searched a good stretch of the slope, crawling on her knees. She had brushed aside dead leaves with her hands and clawed in between tree roots with her fingers, but all to no avail.

She stood up, her back aching, and stretched. Then she brushed the dried earth from her skirt.

With a sigh, she turned back towards the house.

'What have you been doing?' asked Sally in horror, as she caught sight of Catherine's gown. 'You look like you've been playing in the dirt.'

'That's just about right,' said Catherine. 'But it's no use you complaining, Sally. I did what had to be done.'

'And did you find what you were looking for?' asked Sally, as she helped Catherine out of her gown which, despite her best efforts, was noticeably grubby.

Catherine shook her head.

'Ah, well, you'll feel better with some lunch inside you.'

Catherine gave a tired smile. Sally was mothering her, but in her present state of near-exhaustion she did not object.

'You'll be wanting another bath tonight,' said Sally shrewdly, seeing how stiffly Catherine was moving.

She nodded, 'I will.'

However, she made a conscious effort to move gracefully as she joined her fellow guests for luncheon, not wishing them to know that anything was amiss.

Another excursion was being discussed. Whilst Mrs Maltravers scolded Melissa and Miss Dunstan saw to her mother, Mr Spence was suggesting a trip to visit a local beauty spot. The picnic had been enjoyable, and most of the guests were eager to repeat the experience, this time with a different destination. Only Mr Glover demurred.

Finding herself seated beside him, Catherine said, 'You are still grieving over Miss Simpson?'

He answered her in a monosyllable.

Catherine, however, had the feeling he wanted to talk. She turned the conversation to less personal things: stories of Lord Byron's conduct on the Continent, and a discussion of the likelihood of the Regent taking the throne.

Throughout it all, Mr Glover was distracted. Then suddenly he burst out, 'You wonder why I am so upset by Miss Simpson's death? I will tell you why. She was an angel. And her cousin was the same. If only I'd been a minute sooner I could have stopped it. I was there, in the woodland, when she fell. I heard her fall. If only that damned fool hadn't been there too I wouldn't have had to talk to him and then she might have been saved.'

Catherine waited patiently.

'Calls himself a clergyman!' snorted Mr Glover. 'Creeping around in the woodland and accosting people. What was he doing there? That's what I'd like to know. If he'd been in his vicarage where he was supposed to be then I'd have got on with my walk and been there when Miss Winter fell.'

Clergyman? thought Catherine. With an effort she refrained from asking the question she was longing to ask and said instead, 'There was nothing you could have done. Even if you had seen her fall you could not have prevented it.'

'Of course I could. If Amundel had seen someone coming he wouldn't have pushed her in the first place.'

'Lord Amundel didn't —' began Catherine, before cutting herself off. Mr Glover evidently believed, along with everyone else, that Lord Amundel had murdered Miss Winter, and she felt it would be better not to disabuse him of the notion. He was finding it difficult enough to come to terms with the double tragedy, and Catherine dreaded to think what he might do if he realised the murderer was very probably still at large. Fortunately he believed, like most of the house guests, that Miss Simpson's death had been an accident.

Mr Glover stared morosely ahead of him, not noticing her curtailed speech.

'By clergyman, you mean Mr Lucas?' Catherine asked at last.

'Of course I do,' he said irritably. Colouring a moment letter and saying, 'Excuse me. I have forgotten my manners.'

'He was coming to the house?' asked Catherine.

'I don't know,' said Mr Glover without interest.

'Did you meet him coming towards you, or was he going in the same direction?' she asked patiently.

He frowned, focusing on her question. 'He was coming towards me.'

'And you were going which way? Towards the house or away from it?'

'I was going . . . look here, what is all this?' He looked at her suspiciously.

'I was merely curious,' said Catherine lightly.

'Oh, well, if it makes any difference, I was going away from the house. I was taking a stroll before dinner. So he must have been going towards it.'

So. On the night of Miss Winter's death, the Reverend Mr Lucas had been going towards Whitegates Manor. Why?

And did it have anything to do with what Miss Winter had wanted to speak to him about?

She had been inclined to think that Mr Lucas had known nothing about Miss Winter's intention to visit him that evening, but now she was not so sure.

' . . . don't you agree?' asked Mrs Maltravers.

Catherine realised with a start that Mrs Maltravers

was addressing her. 'I beg your pardon?' she said.

'It is an excellent notion to have an excursion, do you not agree?'

'Yes,' said Catherine. She had no idea what the proposed excursion was, but felt it would be good for Mr Glover to get away from Whitegates. And as he showed no inclination to leave, then encouraging him to go on an outing was the next best thing.

It was after luncheon that the idea occurred to her. She had spent a fruitless morning searching the area where Miss Winter had fallen, hoping to find the ring, but she had been foolish. There had been no need for her to go down on her hands and knees and root about in the dirt. By a simple ruse, she could have induced the gardeners to look for it: they had the tools and the time for the job, and did not need to break off their search every time someone walked by.

As soon as she managed to get some time alone she took a walk in the grounds. As usual, a number of gardeners were working there. She chose a young man who, she felt, would be eager to please.

'I wonder if you could help me?' she asked.

The young man, a bony individual with callused hands but an intelligent face, rested on his rake and nodded his head respectfully.

'A friend of mine visited the house some time ago,' she said glibly, 'and she lost her ring. She wasn't able to find it, and resigned herself to its loss, but I would like to surprise her by its return and I wondered whether you might be able to help me.'

'I reckon,' said the young man.

'Let me show you where she thinks she lost it,'

Catherine said. She took him to the appropriate place. 'It may be buried under a pile of leaves, or trapped between some tree roots.'

The young man looked at the slope appraisingly. 'It could do with a clear out, this place, and no mistake. There's leaves here from years ago, I reckon. No one likes to touch it much because of what 'appened.' Unlike Odgers he did not want to shock her and spared her the story, little knowing that she was already acquainted with it. 'I'll see what I can do, miss.'

'Thank you.'

Well pleased with her strategy, Catherine returned to the house. If the ring was there, she had high hopes the gardener would find it. With a full complement of rakes and spades, to say nothing of hoes and forks, he could search the area far more thoroughly than she could do, and even more thoroughly than the murderer would have been able to do. What was more, he could do it without attracting suspicion. Perhaps she may yet find the evidence she needed to shed light on the double murder.

Chapter Fourteen

'I am so glad you are coming to church,' said Lady Carlton.

It was Catherine's first Sunday at Whitegates Manor, and she was standing in the hall waiting for the carriages to be brought round. A fine rain was falling, and the proposed walk to the church had been abandoned. Catherine had been disappointed in this. She had been hoping to see for herself how far it was to the vicarage, how many paths there were, and how long it would take to walk there. However, she contented herself with the fact that she would be able to see the Reverend Mr Lucas in his own habitat. And afterwards she might have an opportunity to talk to him and discover why he had been going to the Manor on the evening of Miss Winter's murder. And whether she had an opportunity to speak to Mr Lucas or not she meant to find time during the week to speak to his housekeeper and see if she could find out whether Miss Winter had in fact visited him on the evening of her death: because Catherine was not inclined to believe his assertion that he had not seen the young lady until she had done everything in her power to verify the fact.

'It is so good to have things returning to normal,' Lady Carlton continued. 'I really do believe we are over the worst.' She looked suddenly conscious stricken. 'Is it wrong of me, do you think, to feel that way?'

Catherine was reassuring. 'No. I think it is natural. You can do nothing about Miss Simpson's death, but you can do a great deal to add to your guests' peace of mind. I think you are right to turn your efforts to that quarter.'

'Thank you, my dear. You are such a comfort. I wonder what is keeping Wilkins?' she added, speaking of the coachman. 'He knows we have to be at the church by - ah! Here he is now.'

The Carlton coach rolled up to the front door. It was a splendid equipage pulled by matched bays. Behind it came a number of smaller carriages, enough to convey the guests to church in comfort, or at least those of the guests who chose to go.

Miss Dunstan helped her mother, who was hobbling painfully, out of the door. Lord and Lady Cuthbertson followed, Lady Cuthbertson declaring that country sermons were never worth listening to and Miss Rivers murmuring, 'Quite so. Oh, yes, indeed it is just so.'

The Thomas boys followed. All three of them, somewhat to Catherine's surprise, were attending church. However, she was not surprised to see that Mrs Maltravers and her daughters were not. Mr Stanton, too, did not appear to be attending.

As they arranged themselves in the various equipages, ably assisted by Lord Carlton, who had stood at the top of the stone steps outside the front door to wait as the carriages were brought round, Catherine found her eyes settling on the Thomas boys.

158

Frederick, who was apparently in love with Felicity Maltravers, and had supposedly been sweet on Miss Winter; Edward, who liked poetry, and Tom. She realised as she smoothed her skirts beneath her that she knew very little about Tom Thomas, and decided to draw him out.

She began by making a commonplace remark about the weather and was pleased to find that he answered her with easy, unaffected manners. He was, she guessed, about one-and-twenty years of age, and whilst he was lively, his liveliness was underpinned by a solidity which Catherine found reassuring. Tom Thomas, she felt, was that rarest of things, an entertaining and yet reliable young man.

'Is this your first visit to Whitegates?' she asked, being pleased that she found herself in a carriage with Miss Dunstan and her mother: Miss Dunstan was busy seeing to her mother's comfort, and Catherine was therefore able to talk to the youngest Mr Thomas undisturbed.

'Yes.'

'And how do you like it?' she asked.

'I like it very well. The country hereabouts is very pretty, and I often spend the summer here - not at Whitegates, but nearby with friends. In fact, it is through those friends that Lady Carlton invited us to Whitegates.'

'Ah, yes, I remember Mr Trevelyan telling me so.' She hesitated, and then said daringly, 'It has not been easy for Lady Carlton, I fear, since Miss Winter's death.'

Mr Thomas looked suitably grave. 'No, indeed.'

'And now it will be even worse.' Her genuine

concern for Lady Carlton was evident in her voice, despite the fact that she had tried to keep her tone light.

He nodded. 'I would like to contradict you, but the world is a predictable place. However, with the party continuing, it is to be hoped that not too much damage will be done. Lady Carlton is charming, and the house is lovely. It would be a shame if an accident spoiled it.'

'An accident,' said Catherine, 'and a murder.'

'As you say. An accident and a murder.'

'Were you here two years ago?' she asked innocently.

'In the neighbourhood? Yes.'

'Oh, yes, of course. I remember Mr Trevelyan saying so. It must have been a terrible shock for Frederick,' she said, somewhat obliquely.

Was she imagining it, or had a wary look come into young Mr Thomas's eye?

'Why so?' he asked.

'Because of his relationship with Miss Winter. But forgive me. I have been indiscreet.'

Some of his ease of manner left him. 'There was no relationship.'

'I thought . . . that is . . . I had heard that your brother was sweet on Miss Winter. But I see that I am wrong.'

'My brother liked her, as he liked many young ladies. He enjoyed her company, but that was all.'

Feeling that she had trespassed on his good nature for long enough she asked him whether he too, like his brother Edward, enjoyed poetry. 'We had a very interesting conversation over dinner one evening, discussing the merits of our favourite poets,' she said.

Mr Thomas relaxed. 'No. Poetry is Edward's passion. I am more interested in outdoor pursuits.'

The rest of the journey passed pleasantly and before long they arrived at the church.

The church was a small but pleasing building, and was in a good state of repair. A neat and orderly churchyard surrounded it, and a lych gate gave it a picturesque feel.

The rain had fortunately stopped, and Lady Carlton's guests were able to proceed through the pretty lych gate and along the gravel path to the church without getting wet.

Once inside, the air of prosperity continued. The mahogany pews were polished, and the church plate shone. Fresh flowers were arranged at the far end and gave a welcome splash of colour. The church was obviously both loved and looked after, and Catherine took her place with a sense of peace that had been missing for her since her arrival at the Manor. It was good to be in a place of tranquillity, where the spirit could restore itself after the troubles of the outside world.

The Reverend Mr Lucas was clearly gratified to see such a large party from Whitegates Manor, as well as his usual congregation of local families, and rose to the occasion splendidly. He preached a sermon that walked a difficult line between dwelling on the unfortunate circumstances at the Manor, which had now leaked out, and ignoring them altogether. Catherine was surprised but pleased at his tact, particularly as she saw the beneficial effect it had on Lady Carlton, who had been labouring under a great strain over the last few days. All in all, she felt much better for her visit to the church, and she was certain her fellow guests felt the same.

'A delightful sermon,' said Lady Carlton to Mr Lucas as he thanked her for coming outside the door. 'Thank you so much.'

'My dear Lady Carlton, I am so glad you are pleased.'

One by one his parishioners thanked him, and Catherine realised it would be impossible for her to get a word with him alone - at least for the moment.

Could a man who had preached such a good sermon, who had written and spoken it with such tact and understanding, be guilty of murder? she asked herself. She did not think so.

But she did not know.

Miss Winter's journal was once again in Catherine's hands. She had reclaimed it from its position at the bottom of one of her drawers and had settled down to read it. Pleading tiredness she had retired early and now sat in her bedchamber, turning over the pages of the journal. When first she had looked into it she had read the early entries in an effort to learn something of Miss Winter's character, and had then moved to the end of the journal, reading the entry for the day she was murdered. But the pages in between she had largely skipped. Now she meant to read the journal through. In particular she wanted to know if there was any mention of Mr Frederick Thomas. He had reputably been sweet on Miss Winter, despite the fact that his brother had denied it, and if Lord Amundel had not given her a ring on that fateful evening, it seemed likely that Frederick Thomas may have done so.

Catherine had wanted to turn the conversation round to jewellery when she had been talking to Tom Thomas that morning, but had not been able to do so. She had tried to think of an innocuous way to introduce the subject but had been defeated. And so she had let the matter rest. But perhaps Miss Winter's journal may mention something about a ring. Perhaps a young man had asked her what sort of rings she favoured, or perhaps she made mention somewhere of being particularly fond of diamonds or rubies.

Catherine began to read.

. . . *the season is exhausting, but so amusing! Really, I don't know what my mother is talking about! She declares that men are aloof creatures to be hunted, and yet it seems they are hunting me! I went out onto the terrace at Lady P's ball, in search of a little air, and Mr Glover tracked me down. Really, he is too silly. He says he loves me and will never love anyone but me. And yet he has only seen me twice! What strange creatures men are!* . . . *Drury Lane was splendid. And Mr Kean! What a splendid Shylock he made! All London is ringing with talk of it! But now, every young man who can hold a quill is fancying himself a playwright. Mr Edmund Spence talked of nothing else when he danced with me this evening. He has written a play, he says, about two star-crossed lovers. He drove me to such distraction that in the end I told him I would applaud his play when I saw it on the stage. And now I am feeling sorry, for by the look in his eyes I could tell I had hurt his feelings and I was really very rude, but oh! to be talked at, instead of to. I am afraid it brought out the worst in me . . .*

Catherine read these entries very closely, and then taking a sheet of notepaper out of her writing-table she proceeded to write very carefully across the page. When she had done she sanded her writing and read it through. Then, satisfied, she returned to the journal. She intended to finish it before she allowed herself to go to bed. With luck, the gardener would find the ring, and if he did so, then would come the tricky part: she would have to discover who it belonged to. She doubted if the murderer would confess to having owned it, and her hope lay in either someone recognising it, or in a clue to its appearance or owner in Miss Winter's journal - a reference to a ring she had been shown, perhaps, or a young man asking her what sort of jewels she preferred.

She turned her attention back to the journal and read assiduously until the candle burned down. She gave an exclamation. Why had she not thought to make sure she had plenty of candles before she began? Now she would have to wait until the following day to finish her work. Still, there was no help for it. Feeling for the edge of the pie-crust table she placed the journal down on it and then made her way carefully into bed.

'You are very quiet this morning.'

Mr Stanton startled Catherine out of her reverie. She was on the lawn, watching the Maltravers girls playing croquet.

'Am I?' she asked vaguely.

He gave her a quizzical look. 'Yes. You are. What are you thinking about?'

'Oh. Nothing.'

'You have discovered something.' He gave her a penetrating look. 'I thought we had agreed to share everything we learnt.'

She felt uncomfortable. They had indeed made such an agreement, but she did not want to tell him her ideas about the ring. There was just a chance it might prove to belong to his brother after all, and until she was sure of its ownership she did not want to mention it to him. 'There's nothing really to share. I came across a number of suggestive entries in Miss Winter's diaries.' She told him about Miss Winter's comments on Mr Glover and Mr Spence, and a further entry she had discovered that morning, detailing an argument with Mrs Maltravers. It appeared that Mrs Maltravers had done everything in her power to turn Miss Winter against Lord Amundel, telling several unsavoury stories about him. But Miss Winter had not been deceived. . . . *she thinks I don't see through her, but she is mistaken. She is trying to turn me against Lord Amundel because she wants him for one of her girls. Or should I say, she wants his money and title for one of her girls . . .* had been the exact entry: Miss Winter, though young, had had a strong personality and had been nobody's fool.

'You may be interested to know that on the evening of Miss Winter's death, Mrs Maltravers had retired to her room with a headache. Mrs Killean remembers it clearly because the weather felt as though thunder was on the way, and one or two of the ladies were indisposed,' said Lord Amundel.

'The Misses Maltravers?' asked Catherine.

Lord Amundel nodded. 'Or at least Clarissa and

165

Melissa. They, too, had retired to their rooms. Felicity spent the evening playing piquet with her hosts.'

'And is Mrs Killean's memory to be trusted? It is a long time ago for her to be sure.'

'I think it is. Miss Winter's death fixed the evening very clearly in her mind.'

'But Mrs Maltravers would not have been able to have a horse saddled or a carriage readied without it being noticed,' said Catherine. 'And nor would the girls.'

'No. But Bellcroft Lodge is not all that far from here. Although the gates to the respective properties are ten miles apart, the actual houses are less than a mile apart.'

'Walking distance,' said Catherine.

'Yes.'

'Even so, if they had walked they would almost certainly have been seen.'

'I agree. Unless, of course, they took pains that they should not. Even then, it is unlikely that any of the Maltravers were involved. We know that Miss Winter was with a man. It was a man's voice, remember, that said he had a ring for her.'

'Unless they had an accomplice.'

'It is possible.'

'Have you been able to discover whether Mrs Maltravers had any financial difficulties? If she had, she may well have been desperate to further a match between your brother and her daughter.'

Catherine had tried to discover whether Mrs Maltravers had been in financial difficulties for herself but had drawn a blank.

'She does not seem to have had any money

troubles. I could not ask outright, of course. Nevertheless, I brought the conversation round to the subject on a number of occasions and as far as I can determine, she is comfortably off.' He paused and then went on. 'And then there are the Thomas boys. The two younger boys have an alibi: Edward and Tom were taking part in charades.'

'And Frederick?'

Lord Amundel hesitated. 'Here the information is unreliable. Mr Trevelyan is of the opinion that Frederick was out riding, but he could not be sure: as you say, it is a long time ago. I did not press him on the point, as I did not want to raise his suspicions.'

'So it seems that Mrs Maltravers, Clarissa or Melissa could have been in the woodland at the time Miss Winter was murdered, although it seems highly unlikely. And Frederick Thomas, certainly if he was out riding, could easily have been there.'

'And what did you discover?' asked Lord Amundel. 'Which of the house guests had an alibi?'

'All of them or none of them - they were all dressing for dinner at the time.'

'Except Mr Glover and Lord Gilstead.'

'That is just the thing. As far as I can gather they were also dressing for dinner.'

'You are saying that your information is unreliable?'

'Exactly,' said Catherine. 'Everyone dressed in their own room. Apart from their own servants they were seen by no one, but that is to be expected.'

'And have you questioned the servants?'

'I asked Sally to see to that. But not all of them have the same servants they had two years ago. Mr

Glover's man has been with him for less than a year. Mr Spence does not have a man and professes to do everything for himself. Lord Cuthbertson's valet is an old family retainer, and he vouched for Lord Cuthbertson - without realising he was doing so, of course. Lady Cuthbertson's maid has been with her for just over a year, and Miss Rivers, of course, does not have a maid, but manages by herself.'

'Which leaves the Carltons.'

'As you say. They were attended by their regular servants. However, as they both had household matters to see to they did not spend long dressing and could have paid a visit to the woodland at any time.'

'And the Reverend Mr Lucas?'

'I have not yet had a chance to speak to his housekeeper, but I will do so tomorrow.'

'Good.'

They watched the croquet together in companionable silence.

'Will you take a turn in the grounds with me?' asked Lord Amundel some five minutes later. 'We have spent almost all our time together talking about murder. I would like to take some time to get to know you better for yourself.'

Catherine felt a sudden *frisson*. Did she really want to get to know Lord Amundel? And to allow him to get to know her? She had a feeling that any greater intimacy between them would be dangerous. But still she found herself saying, 'I would like that,' and then accepting his arm.

'You look happy,' observed Sally.

'Do I?' asked Catherine nonchalantly.

'Yes. You do.'

'I am enjoying my holiday,' replied Catherine.

'Indeed,' remarked Sally.

'Yes,' said Catherine with a mischievous smile.

'I ran into Lord Amundel's man below stairs,' said Sally innocently. 'He seems to think very highly of his master. Galton was Lord Amundel's batman in the war.'

Despite herself - she would much rather have continued with her feigned indifference in front of Sally - Catherine was interested.

'It seems Lord Amundel saved Galton's life.'

Catherine glowed. Why it should matter to her that Lord Amundel was a hero she did not know - or rather she did. Her feelings for him were becoming warmer and more sincere with every passing day. She had spent a delightful hour with him, learning more about his family and telling him a little about hers. They had both of them lost their parents and were living independent lives, going where the fancy took them. But whereas she was enjoying her freedom, which formed such a delightful contrast to the circumscription of her earlier years, she had detected a sense of restlessness in Lord Amundel, as though he was looking for something more.

'A fine gentleman,' said Sally pointedly, recalling Catherine's thoughts.

'Yes. He is.'

'A - what did you say?' asked Sally, mouth agape. She was astonished that Catherine had agreed.

'I said he is.'

Sally's look of astonishment gave way to one of pleasure and then of smugness. 'I was wondering when you'd see it.'

'I saw it the first time I met him. However, there is a very wide gap between a fine gentleman and one I would want to sacrifice my freedom for. If I was married I would not be able to go where I wanted and do as I pleased. I would not have been able to accept Lord and Lady Carlton's invitation to Whitegates, for example, or at least it would have been difficult to do so if my husband had disapproved of the idea. And I may not have been able to walk down to the rectory this afternoon, as I plan to do, and make enquiries about the Reverend Mr Lucas: my husband might have had other ideas.'

'And a good thing, too,' said Sally. 'Getting mixed up in all this murder business isn't good for you.'

'Maybe not. But Miss Winter and Miss Simpson are dead, Sally. And if I turn my back on the fact that their deaths are suspicious, then their murderer may very well kill again.'

Chapter Fifteen

'The rectory?' asked Lady Carlton.

'Yes. I don't know how it happened, but I think I must have left my gloves in the church,' said Catherine. She did not like deceiving Lady Carlton, but she realised that if she was to discover who the murderer was then she would have to be a little devious on occasion, and had decided that the circumstances justified her small deception.

'I can send one of the footmen for you,' volunteered Lady Carlton.

'No. Thank you, there is no need for that. I would like a walk and I might as well have the rectory as a destination.'

'Well, the shortest way is down through the gardens. Cross to the rose gardens, take the path through the woodland, and as you emerge from the trees you will find yourself at a stile. Cross the stile and take the path across the fields. Then turn left onto the road, turn right at the milestone and you are almost there.'

'I think that's what I'll do. Are the other ways much longer?'

'There is only one other way, and that is to go by road. But it is quite a distance, as you will have seen when we drove to church, and the walk is not nearly so pleasant.'

'Then I'll take the path.'

She set off, but not two minutes later was accosted by Lady Cuthbertson. 'Heard you say you were going to the rectory. We can go together.'

Catherine felt her spirits sink. The last thing she wanted was to be accompanied by Lady Cuthbertson, but there was nothing for it, and she and Lady Cuthbertson struck out together.

Lady Cuthbertson was a good walker, with a long stride, and Catherine, who liked to walk briskly herself, was pleased that at least she would not have to loiter on her companion's behalf.

'Mrs Marsden's cottage is just beyond the vicarage, and I told her I would take tea with her this afternoon. She is having a terrible time with one of her maids. Servants these days,' said Lady Cuthbertson, resolutely ignoring the fact that she herself had been little more than a servant a few years before, 'are a sore trial.'

Catherine was relieved that Lady Cuthbertson was not going to the rectory itself. At least, once they reached the cluster of houses that surrounded the church, she and Lady Cuthbertson would part ways.

'Gardeners have been lax again,' said Lady Cuthbertson severely, noticing a plant that had fallen over. She looked slightly put out that Catherine did not murmur, 'Shocking! Oh yes, I do so agree!' as Miss Rivers would have done, but then continued. 'Same everywhere. Riots and trouble - I blame Caroline.'

Catherine, who had been expecting Lady Cuthbertson to name the radicals as the cause of all the problems with rioting and such like, was astonished that Lady Cuthbertson should blame the Regent's wife.

'If she had stuck to her duty as a wife should then none of this would have happened.'

'None of this . . . ?' asked Catherine faintly.

'Set a good example,' declared Lady Cuthbertson. 'That's what she should have done. If Royalty can't set an example then the country's bound to fall apart.'

Catherine felt it was wiser to say nothing. Indeed, she began to see why Miss Rivers found it so easy to agree. Lady Cuthbertson's remarks were so outlandish that to argue with them would have been as useless and absurd as trying to turn the tide.

They walked briskly through the rose garden and into the woodland. They were just going down the sloping path when the young gardener, who was working further along the path, saw them. A smile lit his face.

How unfortunate, thought Catherine. She would really rather he did not make any mention of his search for the ring in front of Lady Cuthbertson. The fewer people who knew about it the better - at least for the time being, until she had discovered who it belonged to. However, it could not be helped.

But the gardener did far more than mention the ring. Walking towards Catherine with a wide grin on his face he said, 'I've found it!'

'You've found it?' asked Catherine, torn between chagrin that Lady Cuthbertson was present and delight that the ring had been found.

'Yes, miss. Caught up in some tree roots it was, under a pile of leaves. But here you are.' And reaching into his pocket he pulled out a ring.

Catherine took it from him, and as she did so she caught sight of Lady Cuthbertson's face. It had gone white. Lady Cuthbertson raised stricken eyes to hers. A faint whisper escaped her. 'Emmy.'

Catherine's chagrin that Lady Cuthbertson was present vanished, and she thanked the fortune that had made Lady Cuthbertson accompany her on her walk down to the vicarage. Lady Cuthbertson had evidently recognised the ring. But her whispered, "Emmy?"

The meaning, though strange, was only too clear. Emmeline Rivers, Lady Cuthbertson's companion. Catherine felt her spirits sink. She had hoped the ring would reveal the identity of the murderer, but if it belonged to Miss Rivers then it was of no use. Miss Rivers could not have given the ring to Miss Winter. The ring had been given by a man.

And then Catherine remembered. Miss Rivers acting in Mr Spence's play. Taking the part of Sir Toby Entwhistle. And performing it with astonishing skill. Catching the walk and voice of a man. All Catherine's preconceived notions slipped away.

Miss Rivers.

The scene played itself out in her imagination as it had done on occasion before, but this time the hand offering the ring to Miss Winters was not a man's hand. It was the hand of Emmeline Rivers.

But why?

Yes, why?

The problem seemed insoluble. Why should Lady Cuthbertson's companion kill Miss Winters? And then Miss Simpson? Although the murder of Miss Simpson was unfortunately only too easily understood: she had been suspicious about her cousin's death, and had

174

been about to discover a clue to the murderer's identity. But still, why kill Miss Winter in the first place? There must be something missing, something Catherine did not yet know. Unless . . . could it be possible? There was just a chance that she had misunderstood Lady Cuthbertson's exclamation, and that the ring did not belong to Miss Rivers at all.

A slight movement brought her attention back to the present. She thanked the gardener for finding the ring, nodded as he beamed, 'My pleasure, miss,' watched him pick up his hoe and return to his tasks further down the path, then turned to Lady Cuthbertson. She was torn between making sure that she had understood Lady Cuthbertson correctly, and not revealing her hand. But her need to know won the day. She turned to Lady Cuthbertson. 'You recognise this ring, don't you?'

'No.' Lady Cuthbertson's voice was forceful and the colour had returned to her cheeks. 'Thought I did but I don't.'

'It belongs to Miss Rivers, doesn't it?'

For the first time since she had known her, Catherine saw Lady Cuthbertson look unsure of herself.

Catherine hesitated, then said, 'Lady Cuthbertson, Miss Winter was murdered —'

'By Amundel,' said Lady Cuthbertson forcefully. 'Nothing to do with Emmy. Nothing at all. Just because she thought a piece of luck might come her way. And why shouldn't it? That's what I'd like to know.'

'Luck? Do you mean Miss Rivers benefited by Miss Winter's death?'

'Certainly not. But saw I'd married well. Wanted the same for herself. And why not? He had a comfortable home. Needed a wife.'

Catherine looked at Lady Cuthbertson in bewilderment. What was she talking about?

And then Mr Glover's words came back to her.

The Reverend Mr Lucas had been in the woodland at the time of Miss Winter's death. What if he had been there to meet Emmeline Rivers? 'You mean Mr Lucas,' she said.

'And why shouldn't she?' demanded Lady Cuthbertson.

'No reason,' said Catherine. 'No reason at all.'

Miss Rivers and Mr Lucas? An idea was forming at the back of Catherine's mind. Could it be that Miss Winter had seen or heard something to discredit one or both of them, and that they had carried out the murder together? She shook her head in confusion. She did not know. But one thing was certain. Her business at the rectory was now more urgent than ever.

'Lady Cuthbertson, I have a favour to ask of you. I cannot go back to the house, but I don't believe Miss Rivers should be left alone.'

'Doesn't need an alibi, if that's what you're thinking,' snorted Lady Cuthbertson. 'There'll be no more murders at Whitegates Manor.'

'Even so, for her own good, I feel Miss Rivers should have someone with her. Will you undertake to keep an eye on her? I would rather it was you than someone else.'

Lady Cuthbertson seemed about to protest further, but then changed her mind. 'Very well. Though it's all nonsense,' she snorted.

'I hope it may be so.'

Catherine tucked the ring away in her reticule. 'I will return to the Manor as soon as I can.'

She watched Lady Cuthbertson depart, and then turned her steps once more towards the rectory.

Miss Rivers and Mr Lucas, she thought. So now she knew *who*. Unless it was simply Miss Rivers? Or only Mr Lucas? But more puzzling was why? Neither of them benefited by Miss Winter's death, at least as far as she knew.

Could Miss Winter, then, have discovered something about one or other of them? Something that could discredit them? But even if she had found out something about them, could it really have been necessary to silence her in such a drastic way? A few weeks more and Miss Winters would have left the Manor and returned to her home.

But then, she had been intending to visit Mr Lucas at the rectory on the evening of her murder. That must have had something to do with it. Did she ever reach the rectory? Was it to forestall her visit that she was killed? Had Mr Lucas been in the woodland in all innocence, and had Miss Rivers killed Miss Winter alone? To prevent the young woman from revealing something about her past to Mr Lucas, which would have put him off the idea of making Miss Rivers his wife?

The walk to the rectory was undemanding, Catherine discovered, turning her attention back to her route and hoping it may give her a further insight into Miss Winter's death. It could be made by anyone of a reasonable standard of fitness, and it was sheltered from view in the woodland, twisting and turning so that it was impossible to see more than a few yards ahead at any one time.

Mr Lucas had seemingly vanished into thin air on the night of Miss Winter's murder - after being seen by Mr Glover he had not been seen again - and Catherine realised how easy it would have been for him to disappear round one of the twists of the path.

A minute's walk would take him out of view of the scene of the murder, and further twists would give him every chance of remaining unseen. Presumably, then, he had retraced his steps to the rectory after the murder, instead of carrying on towards the house. A thing he would not have done if he had been innocent, Catherine felt. Surely it would have been more natural for him to go to the house as he had intended to do? But no. He had simply disappeared.

The Reverend Mr Lucas must have been involved.

Catherine was glad of it. Somehow she did not like to think of Miss Rivers deliberately pushing Miss Winter to her death. Miss Rivers was implicated in the murder because of the ring, it was true, but she could have given it to Mr Lucas in good faith. He could have offered to have had it cleaned for her, or to have had the stone re-set. And then made an excuse as to why it was never returned, safe in the knowledge that the downtrodden Miss Rivers would not question him about it or make a fuss.

But again she came up against the question, why? If Mr Lucas's had been the hand that had pushed Miss Winter, then why did he do it? If indeed he would have had time. She frowned. Of course. His could not have been the hand. He had met Mr Glover in the woodland, which gave him an alibi. He would not have had time to meet Miss Winter, talk to her about the ring and then push her down the slope, in between talking to Mr Glover in the woodland and Mr Glover arriving on the scene - would he? She would have to talk to Mr Glover again and make sure.

The rectory was now in view. Catherine was hoping that Mr Lucas was not at home. Half an hour's conversation with his housekeeper would be useful, and luck was on her side. Mr Lucas had just gone out, the housekeeper said, when Catherine was admitted to the rectory.

'Then I believe I will wait.'

'Very good, miss.'

The housekeeper took her into the small parlour at the back of the house. It was cosily furnished. Catherine sat down, and then detained the housekeeper by saying, 'Have you been with Mr Lucas long?'

The housekeeper looked slightly surprised to be addressed, but answered readily enough. 'Yes, miss. I've been the housekeeper at the rectory for nigh on twenty years.'

'You must have seen a great deal of life in that time. All life passes through a rectory.'

'Yes, miss, that's the truth.'

'I hear you had a Christening here last week?'

'Yes, miss. Mr and Mrs Dunwoody's boy, Jack.'

'Such a happy occasion.' Catherine gave a slight shake of her head. 'Unfortunately, events at the Manor have not been so happy.'

'No, miss.' The housekeeper looked suitably grave.

'This terrible accident. Poor Miss Simpson. And coming on top of the other business. If you have been here for so long you will remember it.'

'Yes, miss. There's those who say the Manor is jinxed. "Nonsense" I tell them. "Heathenish nonsense". Jinxed indeed. Though it is unlucky all the same.'

'Miss Winter visited the rectory, I believe, just before she was killed?'

'I don't know, miss, I'm sure.'

Catherine was disappointed. Although she had no right to be, she told herself. After all, she was discussing events that had taken place two years before.

'Mr Lucas went to the Manor, then?' She caught her breath, wondering whether her question had been too bold.

But the housekeeper was used to answering questions, however strange - indeed, as Mr Lucas's housekeeper, she had answered some far stranger questions put to her by the old biddies of the village. After considering for a moment the housekeeper said, 'Now, let me see. I remember the day because of the tragedy. Mr Lucas had his tea as usual - he always likes his tea at half-past five, unless he's dining out. And then he set about writing his sermon. And then - yes, I remember now. He said he needed a book from the Manor library. Lord Carlton is very generous miss, and lets the Reverend use the library whenever he wants.'

Ah. So that was why he had gone to the Manor - or at least why he had said he had gone to the Manor. But why, then, had he never arrived?

'And did he get the book?'

The housekeeper thought again. 'Why, do you

know, now you come to mention it, I don't think he did. I seem to remember - yes, that's right - he wasn't gone long. He'd just remembered he'd borrowed the book already.' She said to Catherine explainingly, 'Great men are often like that. They forget the silliest things.'

'Ah, yes, of course.' Catherine tried to hide her disappointment. She had hoped her visit to the rectory would provide her with further information, but all it had done was to confirm that the Reverend Mr Lucas had gone to the Manor and had returned shortly afterwards. It could have happened exactly as the housekeeper had remembered it. Perhaps he had really wanted to borrow a book, and then perhaps he had really remembered that he had already borrowed it. Or perhaps it had been no more than a convenient excuse. Well, whichever one it was, it did Catherine no good. Realising there was nothing more for her to learn she said, 'I mustn't take up any more of your time. I really only stopped in to pay my respects as I was visiting the church: I think I left my gloves behind after attending the service and wanted to see if I could find them.'

'I'll tell Mr Lucas you called, miss.'

'Yes, thank you.'

'You should find the verger in the church, miss. He will help you look for your gloves.'

Catherine thanked the housekeeper again and then took her leave. She did indeed call in at the church and ask the verger to help her look for her gloves, which she managed to "find" under one of the pews. And then she returned to the Manor with her most important question unanswered.

Why?

Chapter Sixteen

Catherine was tired, both physically and mentally, by the time the Manor came in sight. Who was the likeliest murderer, she wondered? Miss Rivers or Mr Lucas? She was close to discovering the identity of the murderer, but almost wished she wasn't. She had taken to Miss Rivers who, despite her fussy ways, seemed to be an inoffensive and good-natured woman. And now she had to face the fact that Miss Rivers was possibly a murderer who had killed, not once, but twice.

She felt sick of the whole business.

A part of her wished that she had never become involved; but another part knew that a murderer could not be allowed to go free, lest they should kill again.

Still, she had had enough of it for one evening. She could do no more for the present. The matter of the ring was suggestive but it was not conclusive. Miss Rivers may be the murderer or she may not. She may simply have lost the ring and never known to what use it had been put. She may be completely innocent.

Tomorrow, thought Catherine, I must set about finding more proof. Real, solid, incontrovertible proof. And I must ask Mr Stanton to help me. But for tonight I want nothing more than a hot meal, a bath and an early night.

She crossed the lawn to the house and went in by the side door. As she did so, she passed Lord Gilstead. He looked as though he was about to speak to her on a matter of gravity, but then appeared to think better of it and passed her by.

Good, thought Catherine. She did not want anything more to think about tonight.

She went into the house - and immediately had the feeling that something was wrong. There was a hush, an unnatural stillness, and she was suddenly afraid. Something had happened. Lady Cuthbertson -

She felt a sudden rush of energy, and picking up her skirts ran towards the stairs. To meet Lady Carlton coming down them looking old and grey.

'Oh, Catherine!' she said, her face gaunt, 'how can it have happened? There has been another - I hesitate to call it an accident. And yet that is what it appears to be. But two accidents. . .'

'Lady Cuthbertson —' said Catherine, with icy fingers clutching at her heart. She had asked Lady Cuthbertson to watch Miss Rivers, and by so doing had sent her to her death.

Lady Carlton nodded hopelessly. 'Distraught.'

'I should never have - what? What did you say?'

Lady Carlton looked taken aback. 'I said that Lady Cuthbertson is distraught. I know what you are thinking. You are thinking that she was a hard taskmaster and led her companion a merry dance. But, you know, the two of them were at school together and I believe they were very close.'

Catherine's head was spinning. What was Lady Carlton talking about? She took a deep breath. 'I think you had better tell me what has happened.' She led

Lady Carlton into a small sitting-room which was mercifully unoccupied. 'Now, tell me all about it.'

Lady Carlton sank down on a gilded sofa. She wrung her hands and then plucked at her silk skirts before finally gathering her thoughts and beginning to speak.

'It was Mr Spence who found her.'

Mr Spence, thought Catherine, noting the fact without even realising she was doing so.

Lady Carlton nodded. 'Yes. You see, he needed some air - working out his play, as he said - before dinner. He took a walk along the terrace. And that was when he found her.'

'Found who?' asked Catherine, wanting to be quite clear.

'Hm?' Lady Carlton looked at Catherine as though she had lost the thread of the conversation.

'Found who?' repeated Catherine gently. 'Who did he find?'

'Oh, yes, of course, how silly of me. Miss Rivers. It was poor Miss Rivers, with her head all . . . it was dreadful. It really was. It was all too dreadful. And poor Lady Cuthbertson. She had just been looking for Miss Rivers. She had been up to her room - why she wanted her I don't know - and saw her from the window, walking along the terrace. She went downstairs, but by the time she reached the terrace it had already happened.' Lady Carlton shook her head in despair.

'What had already happened?' asked Catherine.

'The accident.'

Catherine waited, then asked, 'Which was?'

'One of the stone balls. It had crashed down from

the roof. Miss Rivers was underneath . . . '

Catherine felt slightly sick. The roofline was decorated by heavy stone balls. One of them had evidently broken loose, with disastrous results. And yet, it was as Lady Carlton said. Surely it could not have been an accident?

No. Of course not. The first two deaths had not been accidents. She knew that. They had been murders. This, too, must be a murder. And Catherine knew who the most likely suspect was: the Reverend Mr Lucas.

But why? What was his motive for the murders? Did he know that the ring had been found? she wondered suddenly. If so, that would give him the perfect motive for murdering Miss Rivers, if she had given or lent him the ring: so that she could not say so.

'I must go and see Lady Cuthbertson,' she said.

'Oh, my dear, would you? That is very kind of you. I am sure she would appreciate it. She is quite distraught.'

'Where is she?' asked Catherine.

'In her room.'

'I'll go to her now.' She hesitated. 'Is there anything I can get you?'

Lady Carlton managed a weak smile. 'No. Thank you. Nothing.' She stood up. 'I must be getting back to my guests.'

Catherine admired her bravery. But she had no time at the present to do more. She needed to find Lady Cuthbertson, and discover who she had told about the ring. Because someone - the Reverend Mr Lucas - had obviously found the information dangerous, and had silenced Miss Rivers once and for all.

Catherine made her way upstairs. As she did so a wave of weariness washed over her. But she had no time for it. She had to speak to Lady Cuthbertson.

She did not hesitate but, as soon as she reached it, she knocked on Lady Cuthbertson's door. It was answered by a neat maid, who declared that Lady Cuthbertson was resting and was not to be disturbed. But on hearing Catherine's voice, Lady Cuthbertson called, 'Miss Morton. Thank God! Come in.'

Catherine went into the room. Lady Cuthbertson had obviously been resting on the bed: there was an impression on top of the coverlet where she had lain. But now she was sitting in a chair next to the fireplace.

'I must speak to you. Alone,' said Catherine.

'Thank you, Jenkins, that will be all,' said Lady Cuthbertson.

A minute later and the two ladies were by themselves.

'You've heard about Emmy?' Lady Cuthbertson asked.

Catherine nodded. 'I've been a fool. I thought she was the murderer. But it seems as though I was wrong.'

Lady Cuthbertson nodded. 'I knew Emmy could never have killed anyone. And now she is dead. But why?'

'Who did you tell about the ring?' asked Catherine.

Lady Cuthbertson shook her head. 'No one.'

'You are quite sure?'

'Yes. Quite sure.'

'Then it can't be that,' said Catherine.

Lady Cuthbertson looked at her enquiringly.

'I thought that was why she had been killed,' Catherine explained. 'Because the murderer knew that the ring had been discovered and was afraid that, when asked, Miss Rivers would reveal that she had given or lent it to them; if it had been lent, they probably apologised for its loss.'

'Mr Lucas,' said Lady Cuthbertson.

Catherine nodded. He had certainly not been at the rectory that afternoon. But then, if Lady Cuthbertson had not told him, neither had he known that the ring had been found. If he was the murderer then, for all he knew, he was still safe.

Unless . . .

Catherine had a sudden vision of the gardener handing her the ring. It had been in the woodland, on the path to the rectory. If the Reverend Lucas had been there, hidden by a bend in the path, he would have overheard everything. There was nothing for it. She would have to make close enquiries into his movements as soon as she had a chance. But for now she could do no more.

'Say nothing of this to anyone,' said Catherine. 'We will find out who did this, never fear, and we will bring them to book.'

Lady Cuthbertson nodded. 'I hope so.'

'But now I must go and dress. And you must do the same. We can't let Lady Carlton down.'

'No. You are right. Life must go on.'

Lady Cuthbertson straightened her shoulders.

Catherine left her, going straight to her own room.

'I expect you've heard,' said Sally.

'Yes.' Catherine sank down onto the bed.

'You won't be dressing for dinner, then?'

'Yes. I will. We must keep a semblance of normal life going. Lady Carlton cannot be forever sending trays to our rooms.'

Sally nodded. 'Yes. You're right. I'll lay out something sombre.'

'Thank you, Sally.'

Bathed and dressed, Catherine felt a little more able to face the coming evening. She was sure the guests would retire early, but meant to help Lady Carlton through the difficult hours until then. Besides, she wanted to speak to Mr Stanton. If his valet was trustworthy, she wanted to ask him to set the man to watching the rectory. If her suspicions were correct, then the Reverend Mr Lucas must be kept under observation at all times.

But the thing that still puzzled her was, why? Presumably Miss Rivers had been killed because she knew who had killed Miss Winter, even though she may not have realised she knew, because she had given or lent them the ring. She had therefore become a liability to the murderer. And Miss Simpson had been killed because she had been searching for the ring. But why had Miss Winter been killed? What had she discovered that had been so damaging? Why had Mr Lucas been driven to kill? If she could find the answer to this she would be able to set about finding the evidence to prove it. But she was still working in the dark.

She felt a pang as she thought of poor Miss Rivers. Had the elderly spinster known that her ring was the one used to put Miss Winter off her guard? Perhaps, perhaps not. Had she given it to the Reverend Mr Lucas, or had she merely lent it? Or had she even

---

189

simply discovered it was missing, realising later that he had taken it. Had he then made love to her to keep her quiet? Promising that they would one day marry?

These were questions to which she had no answers. Yet.

But she meant to find them.

Starting tonight.

The drawing-room was surprisingly full. Catherine had feared that many of the guests might have requested a tray in their room, but that was not the case. However, there were murmurs and whisperings, and Catherine felt the house party would not long survive this new calamity. And perhaps it was just as well, for who knew when the murderer would strike again? Which made it imperative she find the proof she needed.

She walked over to the fireplace. Old Mrs Dunstan was sitting next to it, a shawl over her knees.

'Nonsense,' she was saying to her daughter. 'It's Miss Simpson who was killed, not Miss Rivers. You're getting as bad as I am.'

Mrs Maltravers, seated in the middle of the room, was scolding her daughters. 'Clarissa, why ever did you wear that gown? And Melissa, what are you doing with that fan? Surely you know better than to scrunch it up like that. The lace will not stand it.'

Whilst Frederick Thomas was hanging over Felicity murmuring, 'It's all right, Felicity, really it is.'

But where was she to go for evidence? thought Catherine, and what -

And all of a sudden it hit her. It hit her with such a blinding flash of clarity that she almost slumped into a nearby chair. Of course. Why had she not seen it before?

She shook her head in amazement. It was all so simple. And at last she knew. Not only who, but why.

'Are you all right?' came a concerned voice at her elbow.

She looked up to see Mr Stanton standing over her.

'I saw you sink,' he said. And then he noticed something in her face. 'You know something, don't you?'

She nodded. 'I do. I must speak to you after dinner. Alone.'

He nodded. 'Very well. But for now, will you accept my arm?'

'Yes, thank you. Gladly.'

The doors were thrown open, and they went into dinner.

'Now, what have you found out?'

'That is something I can't tell you,' said Catherine.

They were in the library, having agreed to meet there once everyone else had gone to bed. Mindful of the fact that she had overheard a conversation in the library before, Catherine had checked the room thoroughly to make sure that she and Mr Stanton were alone before beginning.

'And why not?'

'Because I'm not yet sure. That is, I'm sure in my own mind, but I don't have any proof. And until I have it I don't want to make accusations I can't substantiate.'

'I applaud your motive, but I am not happy about it. Don't forget, our murderer has killed three times already.'

'I have already written a full account of my suspicions - I wrote it after dinner, before I came down to the library to meet you - and if anything should happen to me Sally will give it to you. But I am unwilling to say more until I have the proof I need. And that is something I hope you are going to be able to help me with. Tell me, have you any servants you trust implicitly?'

'My man,' he said promptly. 'He was with me in the war. I would trust him with my life.'

'Good. Then there a number of things I would like him to do. These are errands I cannot run myself. And I would like him to do them now, tonight. They will take some time, and I want to have the evidence I need by lunchtime tomorrow at the latest. The guests are growing restive, and if I don't miss my guess they will be leaving tomorrow or soon after. This matter must be sorted out by then.'

'Very well.'

She told him what she needed to know. He raised his eyebrows, but said nothing. Her requests were odd, but it was clear she thought they were important, and so he agreed to have his valet do everything she asked.

'And then?' he asked.

'And then I must find a way of trapping the murderer.'

Chapter Seventeen

'Lady Cuthbertson, I need your help.'

It was the following morning, and Catherine found Lady Cuthbertson in the drawing-room.

'Yes?' Lady Cuthbertson seemed somewhat listless, but otherwise all right.

'Yes. You see, I believe I know who killed Miss Rivers. But in order to prove it I need your assistance.'

'Anything I can do,' she said more vigorously.

'With Miss Rivers dead, you are the only person who can identify the ring, and it is the ring which is crucial. Will you vouch for the fact that it belonged to Miss Rivers?'

'Yes. Yes, of course.'

'And also vouch for where it was found? I can ask the gardener to vouch for it, of course, but the word of Lady Cuthbertson will carry more weight.'

She seemed to call her mind back from a great distance. 'Yes. Of course.'

'Thank you.'

Having established that Lady Cuthbertson would play her part, Catherine went next to Lord Carlton. He, poor man, had been up half the night. First there had been the unpleasant matter of seeing to Miss Rivers' body, and then checking the roof to see how the stone ball could have come loose. All the other stone balls were checked, but they were all secure.

'I still don't understand how it could have happened,' said Lord Carlton to Catherine, running his hand through his hair.

'Unless it was pushed.'

He shook his head. 'There is no evidence of foul play. Still, two fatal accidents in a matter of days —'

'But they weren't accidents,' said Catherine. 'They were murder.'

'We have discussed this before —'

'But this time it is different. This time I know.'

'What?' he looked up at her with eyes that were suddenly sharp. 'You're saying you know who did this?'

'Yes.'

'Well?' he demanded. 'Who?'

'If I tell you now you will say it is preposterous. Also, there are one or two elements that I cannot yet prove. But —'

He help up his hand. 'Say no more. I know you mean well, but —'

'But the murderer will prove them for me,' she cut across him. 'I have thought of a way to trap the person responsible into an admission. Believe me, Lord Carlton, I am sure. And that is why I am here. I want you to arrange a meeting of all the guests immediately after lunch today. And I want the Reverend Mr Lucas to be there.'

'Lucas? Surely you don't think Lucas —'

'I would simply like him to be there.'

He looked at her dubiously.

'Please.'

He sighed. 'I don't like it, Catherine. But you've

always had a good head on your shoulders. Very well. I will do as you ask.'

'Thank you.'

And then she went to see Mr Stanton.

'It is all arranged,' she said.

'The answers to your queries were what you expected them to be?'

'Yes. Now this is what I would like you to do.'

It was a wary group that assembled in the drawing-room that afternoon. Catherine had taken her place early, and was sitting in the corner when the rest of the guests arrived. Mr Glover was the first to enter. He looked surly and morose. Did he really care about Miss Winter and Miss Simpson? Catherine wondered. Or was it just a pose?

She watched him take a seat by the fireplace and then turned to see Miss Dunstan and her mother come in.

'But I don't want to go into the drawing-room,' Mrs Dunstan was saying. 'I want to go outside.'

'Later, mother. Lord Carlton would just like a word with us first.'

Miss Dunstan helped her mother to sit down on the other side of the fireplace and pulled up an x-framed stool so that she could sit next to her.

'If the girls want to take a walk by the lake I don't see why they should be dragged into the drawing-room,' Mrs Maltravers was saying as she entered on the arm of Lord Amundel. 'Do you?'

Lord Amundel glanced at Catherine and gave her a speaking look.

'I don't believe Lord Carlton will keep us long,' he

said soothingly.

'I should think not. Felicity, what are you doing? What are you and Mr Thomas talking about? Come over here, Felicity, and bring Mr Thomas with you. And his brothers, of course.'

Having thus ensnared the Thomas boys she settled herself down on a splendid sofa, arranging her skirts around her and patting the seat next to her invitingly. 'Dear Mr Stanton,' said Mrs Maltravers who, like most of the guests, was not aware of his true identity, 'you have been such a help. It wouldn't be seemly of me to send you away now. Do, pray, take a seat by me.'

Lord Amundel obligingly sat down, and the three Maltravers girls, flanked by the three Thomas boys, all sat nearby.

Mr Spence was next. He was holding a handkerchief to his face in a suitably flamboyant manner. He was wearing an expression that Catherine guessed was meant to represent tragedy. But behind the handkerchief, his eyes were alert.

Lord Gilstead came in, and with him the Reverend Mr Lucas. Catherine let out her breath. So he was there. He had come. Behind them came Lord and Lady Cuthbertson, Lady Cuthbertson giving a nod of understanding, and Lord and Lady Carlton brought up the rear.

Softly, Lord Carlton closed the doors behind him. And Catherine knew that outside the doors stood six sturdy footmen, who had orders to let no one leave.

'First of all,' said Lord Carlton, standing in the middle of the room and addressing the gathered guests, 'I would like to thank you all for assembling here this afternoon. As you know, we have had two very unfortunate accidents at Whitegates Manor in the last week. At first that was what they seemed to be: tragic accidents. But I'm afraid that evidence has come to light that proves they were not accidents at all. They were acts of murder.'

The faces around him showed a variety of expressions. Mr Glover went bright red and fingered his collar; Mr Spence dropped his handkerchief; Felicity Maltravers gave a small sob and was comforted by Frederick Thomas, whilst Clarissa looked incredulous, Melissa looked excited, Mr Edward Thomas looked shocked and Tom Thomas looked dumbfounded.

'Murder?' asked Mrs Maltravers. 'Nonsense. My dear Lord Carlton, I don't know how you could think such a thing.'

'Hah! So it's murder, is it?' piped up old Mrs Dunstan. 'Why didn't you say so in the first place?'

'Mother!' exclaimed Miss Dunstan.

Lady Cuthbertson nodded, whilst Lord Cuthbertson looked frightened and put his hands between his knees.

Lord Gilstead glanced at Lord Amundel, who looked determinedly ahead of him, whilst the Reverend Mr Lucas mopped his heavily perspiring face.

Lady Cuthbertson noticed Mr Lucas's perspiring, and with a slight nod drew Catherine's attention to it. Catherine nodded in reply.

Lady Carlton, looking grey and old, folded her hands in her lap.

Lord Carlton turned to Catherine. 'Miss Morton? I

believe you have something you wanted to say?'

Catherine nodded. All eyes turned to her.

'I was delighted when Lord and Lady Carlton kindly invited me to Whitegates Manor, as I am sure we all were. But when I spoke of visiting here, the first words I heard were ominous. "Whitegates?" one of my friends asked. "But isn't that where . . . ?" Where what, I wanted to ask. But the conversation moved in a different direction and I put it from my mind. Until, on arriving here, I discovered that Miss Winter had fallen to her death, and that it had not been an accident, but murder.'

'A bad business,' said Mr Spence. 'These lovers' quarrels . . . ' He shrugged.

'A bad business,' Catherine agreed. 'but not a lovers' quarrel.'

'Oh, come now,' said Mr Spence. 'Everyone knows it was Amundel that killed her. Why, he confessed. Just before he blew out his brains.'

'My brother did not confess to killing Miss Simpson,' came Lord Amundel's voice. It was quiet and unemotional.

'Your *brother*?' asked Mr Spence, as a group of astonished eyes turned to Lord Amundel.

'Yes. My brother.'

'Oh, Mr Stanton, that means . . . ' gasped Mrs Maltravers, her eyes shining. '*You* are the new Lord Amundel.'

He gave her a small, ironical bow.

'Girls, isn't this wonderful news? Mr Stanton is a lord.' She beamed at him, oblivious to the fact that they were all assembled to discuss a matter of murder, and in her mind's eye measured him up for his wedding clothes.

'Well, I never,' said Miss Dunstan, whilst her mother gave a shout of 'Ha!'

'You've taken us all for fools, it seems,' said Mr Glover belligerently.

'Given that I knew my brother to be innocent, and that Miss Winter's murderer was still at large, I felt it wiser not to use my title in case the murderer suspected I was not satisfied with the notion of my brother's guilt,' said Lord Amundel evenly.

'We have only your word for it he was innocent,' said Tom Thomas. 'The way I heard it, he said he couldn't live with the guilt.'

Lord Amundel turned towards the young man. 'No more he could. But his guilt was at being late for his appointment with Miss Winter, and not because he had killed her. If he had been on time, she would not have been alone and the murderer would not have had a chance to strike.'

'So, then,' said old Mrs Dunstan, whose eyes had brightened considerably, and who gave every appearance of enjoying herself, 'who did kill her?'

'That is something that troubled Miss Simpson,' said Lord Amundel. 'She did not believe that my brother had murdered her cousin. And she wanted to find out the truth. Which is why she asked Lady Carlton if she could visit Whitegates Manor, to look for some of her cousin's things.'

'So that is why she came!' exclaimed the Reverend Mr Lucas.

All eyes turned towards him.

'I only wondered . . . ' he blustered. 'It seemed such a strange thing to do.' He mopped his forehead again. His handkerchief was wet. 'Her cousin had been killed here. Why would she want to come back again?'

'So that's why,' murmured Mr Glover under his breath.

'Yes. That is why,' said Catherine.

'And then she, too, was murdered,' said Lord Gilstead.

'What makes you say that?' asked Mrs Maltravers sharply.

'Her cousin was murdered, she was dissatisfied with the conclusions drawn, and then she too met with an accident. Even at the time, her death must have been suspicious. In the light of recent events, I would say that her death was certainly murder.'

'I don't see that it follows,' said Mr Glover belligerently.

'But it does,' said Catherine. 'You see, the falling picture was not the only "accident" to befall Miss Simpson. She had already almost been the victim of another one.'

'What? What's that you say?' asked Mrs Dunstan. 'Another accident? I didn't hear anything about another accident.'

'No one heard anything about it, except myself,' said Catherine. 'Because, you see, Miss Simpson thought it was I who was trying to kill her.'

'You?' asked Lady Carlton, astonished.

Mrs Maltravers nodded self-righteously and gave a sideways glance at Lord Amundel, her thoughts plainly written across her face. If Miss Morton turned out to be a murderer, Lord Amundel would have to look elsewhere. And where better to look than in the direction of her three unmarried daughters? She had been cheated of an Amundel once, but she did not intend to lose out again.

'Yes.' Catherine nodded. 'She came into my room shortly after my arrival here and pulled out a pistol. She told me she knew it was me. I had no idea what she was talking about. Fortunately my maid entered the room and Miss Simpson, hiding the pistol in her skirts, left, but after she had gone I made some enquiries. Its seemed she had been accusing me of trying to kill her, and it seemed as though her accusations had had something to do with her morning ride, so I went out to the stables and questioned the grooms. But none of them had seen or heard anything unusual. Then I decided to go for a ride myself. As soon as I picked up my saddle I knew what Miss Simpson had been talking about: the girth of my saddle had been almost cut through. And I had offered to lend it to her.'

'So she thought you'd cut the girth on purpose and then lent it to her, hoping she wouldn't notice and would take a fall,' said Mr Spence, once again sitting forward on his seat.

'Yes.'

'And did you?'

'That's enough, Spence,' said Lord Carlton.

But Catherine answered him anyway. 'No. I did not. But someone did. I thought at first it may have been the work of a disgruntled stablehand or a mischievous child, but I discovered that Lord Carlton's servants are happy and that there are no likely pranksters in the neighbourhood. And then Miss Simpson was the victim of another "accident". Only this time she was killed.'

'It does seem . . . ' said Mr Frederick Thomas with a frown.

His brother, Edward, nodded heavily. 'Yes, it does.'

Tom shifted in his seat.

'But you said Miss Simpson's death was an accident.' The Reverend Mr Lucas turned appealingly to Lord Carlton.

'She was killed by a falling picture. It could have been an accident, or murder. Either way there was no proof.'

'But the cut saddle . . . ' said Miss Dunstan hesitantly.

'Suggestive,' said Lord Carlton. 'But not proof.'

'And that was what I wanted to find,' said Catherine. 'The more I thought about it the more I was convinced that Miss Simpson's death was not an accident. And, as she had come to Whitegates to investigate the death of her cousin, I thought it likely that the two deaths were linked. What was it that made Miss Simpson dangerous? She had come to Whitegates Manor to look for something, Lady Carlton had told me. So what could prove dangerous to the murderer if found? I racked my brains, and at last it came to me. The ring.'

'The ring!' The exclamation appeared to be torn from the Reverend Mr Lucas.

'Yes. The ring.'

'Eh?' asked old Mrs Dunstan. 'What's she talking about, the ring?'

'I don't know, mother,' said Miss Dunstan.

'When Miss Winter fell to her death, her final

conversation was overheard. A man's voice offered her a ring and she took it, exclaiming on its beauty. That was what led people to suspect Lord Amundel. It was well know that he intended to propose to her. The man was assumed to have been Lord Amundel, and the ring in question was assumed to have been an engagement ring. But why should a man murder the young lady he was in the middle of proposing to?'

'You have a point there,' said Mr Spence, his handkerchief and his affected manners forgotten for the moment.

'Miss Simpson was obviously not satisfied. And it obviously occurred to her, somewhere on the way, that there was no ring. All her cousin's effects were returned. But there was no strange ring.'

'What's that got to do with it?' asked Mr Glover.

Catherine turned a penetrating glance on him. 'Miss Winter had just been given a ring when she was pushed to her death. But no ring was found amongst her effects. The fact troubled Miss Simpson. It may have had nothing to do with it; it may have had everything to do with it. But obviously Miss Simpson thought it was important - important enough to prompt her to invite herself to Whitegates Manor. I suspect she wanted to discover whether it had in fact belonged to Lord Amundel. If it had - if it had been a family heirloom - then she would have put aside her doubts and concluded that Lord Amundel had indeed killed her cousin. But if not . . . '

'And have you found it? This ring?' asked the Reverend Mr Lucas. He was still perspiring heavily.

'Yes,' said Catherine. 'I have.'

There was a sudden tension in the room. Mr

Glover ran his finger round the inside of his cravat; the Reverend Mr Lucas wiped his forehead again with his wet handkerchief; Lord Cuthbertson looked as though he was about to cry.

Catherine opened her reticule, and took out the ring. She laid it on the palm of her hand. 'This is the ring. It was found by one of the gardeners on the slope where Miss Winter died.'

'We've only got your word for that,' said Tom Thomas suddenly.

'No.' Lady Cuthbertson's voice rang out. 'Mine as well. Saw it with my own eyes. The gardener found it on the slope all right.'

Catherine nodded.

'And?' asked Mr Spence, leaning even further forward. 'Whose is it?'

'Lady Cuthbertson?' asked Catherine.

'It belonged to Emmy. Miss Rivers.'

Mrs Maltravers looked startled; Lady Carlton perplexed; and Miss Dunstan sighed.

'But . . . ' said Melissa Maltravers nervously. 'Miss Rivers is dead.'

'I know.' Catherine nodded. 'Murdered. And by the same person who murdered Miss Winter and Miss Simpson. When the gardener - at my request - looked for, and found the ring, and when Lady Maltravers identified it, I thought I had found the murderer.'

'No.' It was Lord Gilstead who spoke. 'The other voice was a man's. The conversation that was overheard,' he explained. 'It took place between Miss Winter and a man.'

'A good point. And one which presented a stumbling block,' admitted Catherine. 'Until I remembered Miss Rivers' performance in Mr Spence's play.'

'By God! You're right!' declared Mr Spence. 'She made a most convincing man. But why did she do it?' he added, perplexed.

'That was what I asked myself. Why did she do it? And I could think of no satisfactory reply. And then all of a sudden it came to me. And it was all thanks to Mrs Maltravers.'

Mrs Maltravers nearly dropped her fan in astonishment. 'Me?'

'Yes. You.'

'But how did I . . . ?'

'By scolding Melissa. "Melissa," you said, "what are you doing with that fan? Surely you know better than to scrunch it up like that?"'

'Well, I'm glad to have solved the mystery, to be sure, but I still don't see how . . . ' said Mrs Maltravers.

'Because your words lingered in my mind, and somewhere, somehow, they struck a chord. Where had I heard those words before? I wondered. And how did they hold the key? And then I saw it. I saw it all. The murderer, the reasons for the murders —'

'Well?' demanded Mr Spence.

'It was in the words. " . . . what are you doing with that fan? Surely you know better than . . . Fan. Surely. Fan. Sure. Fanshaw. And I knew I had heard that name before. I had heard of it in two contexts. One, I had heard of it from Miss Rivers - Lady Cuthbertson's maiden name was Fanshaw —'

'What of it?' demanded Lady Cuthbertson. 'Everyone knows my name was Fanshaw.'

'Oh, yes,' said Lord Cuthbertson, speaking for the first time Catherine could remember. 'Elaine's name was Fanshaw.'

'And I had heard - or rather seen - the name elsewhere. In Miss Winter's journal. You see, Miss Simpson had brought her cousin's journal with her, and after her death I took the liberty of reading it. The early entries were of little interest. They were the usual schoolgirl complaints: *Miss Travis is perfectly horrible - she makes me play the pianoforte until my fingers ache and will not seem to realise that I am no more musical than the housemaid's cat . . . Miss Fanshaw is a monster - she takes me out in all weathers, and speaks of fresh air and exercise in the reverent tone Father reserves for his port . . .* '

'Well?' demanded Lady Cuthbertson.

'You were a governess before you married Lord Cuthbertson, were you not?' asked Catherine.

'And proud of it,' said Lady Cuthbertson.

'Were you the same Miss Fanshaw who taught Miss Winter?' asked Catherine innocently.

Lady Cuthbertson hesitated a second. 'Well, what of it?' she asked. 'Everyone knows I was a governess. No shame in that.'

'No indeed. That's what I thought. Even if it's the same Miss Fanshaw, I thought, why would she have wanted to kill Miss Winter? If Lord Cuthbertson had not known about her humble origins, then perhaps it might have been a motive for murder, as she would not have wanted to be disgraced.' She turned to Lady Cuthbertson. 'But Lord Cuthbertson had known all along that you were a governess - indeed, he had employed you to look after his half-brother. So, although there was a previous connection between you and Miss Winter, why should you want to kill her? And then it came to me. *Miss Fanshaw speaks of fresh air and exercise in the reverent tone Father reserves for his port.* An outdoor woman who loved exercise. And yet one who could not swim. You cannot swim, can you, Lady Cuthbertson?'

Again a second's hesitation.

'Now, see here,' said Lord Cuthbertson, finally stirred to make some sort of remonstrance.

'Can you swim, Lady Cuthbertson?'

'No.' Her eyes were sharp.

'No. Of course not. Otherwise you would have rescued little Johnny when he fell into the lake.' There was a deathly hush. 'But of course, you cannot swim. Miss Rivers told me so herself.'

'Good old Emmy,' Lady Cuthbertson sighed.

At this, Catherine's voice became steely. 'Which left you without a motive for murdering Miss Winter. Unless, since leaving school, where you had known Miss Rivers, you had learnt to swim. And had taught Miss Winter to do the same. Then she would have known something about you that you could not afford to have known: that you could swim. That you could have rescued little Johnny when he fell into the lake, but that you chose not to do so; that you had deliberately let Lord Cuthbertson's half-brother drown. Which gave you a motive for killing her. A very powerful motive. To protect your guilty secret. '

'Nonsense,' declared Lady Cuthbertson uneasily. 'Why would I have let Johnny drown?'

'Because you knew that, if Lord Cuthbertson needed an heir, he would have to marry. You also knew he was a quiet man who hated

leaving his estate. And you knew that, if he needed a wife, he would in all probability turn to the nearest available female: you.'

Lord Cuthbertson looked from Catherine to his wife in confusion.

'Balderdash,' said Lady Cuthbertson in a steel to match Catherine's own. 'As you said yourself, I cannot swim, so the rest is a faradiddle.'

'Is it so?' Catherine took something out of her reticule. 'I have here a letter from Mr and Mrs Winter. *My dear Miss Morton - I do not know why you want to know, but yes, Miss Fanshaw was an excellent swimmer.*'

Lady Cuthbertson blanched.

Lord Cuthbertson turned to her uncomprehendingly. 'Elaine?'

His plea seemed to rouse her. She threw back her head. 'Nonsense,' she declared, eyes glittering. 'She is thinking of someone else. Ladies never pay any attention to their governesses. They treat them like pieces of furniture. And I should know. It was the next governess who could swim, or the one before. Besides, even if I killed Miss Winter - which I certainly did not - then why would I kill Miss Simpson and my dear Emmeline?'

'Because Miss Simpson was looking for the ring, and you could not allow her to find it. You had looked for it yourself, after you had pushed Miss Winter to her death, without avail. Even so, you could not take the risk that it might come to light. Because the ring did not belong to Emmeline Rivers. It belonged to you.'

'Nonsense. I've already told you. The ring belonged to Emmy.'

'So I believed. Until I realised I had only your word for it. Even then I could not think why you would lie . . . unless the ring belonged to you. Once I realised that, things began to fall into place. When the gardener handed it to me you knew you had to act quickly to stop your guilt being discovered. If we had been alone I suspect I would have been the next victim of an "accident". But the gardener was present, and I was safe. And so, as you could not silence me, you decided to pretend the ring belonged to Miss Rivers, deliberately focusing suspicion on her. But then you had to silence her. Because otherwise, when asked, she would have declared, quite rightly, that the ring belonged to you.'

'Nonsense,' snorted Lady Cuthbertson.

'Is it?' asked Catherine.

She nodded to Lord Amundel, who walked over to the side of the room and drew something out from behind a chair. It was a portrait of Lady Cuthbertson. And there, clearly visible on her hand, was the ring.

'I . . . borrowed it for the portrait,' said Lady Cuthbertson, licking her lips and looking uneasily round her as if seeking for a means of escape.

'Miss Rivers' ring would not have fit you,' said Catherine. 'Her fingers were the fingers of a needlewoman. They were long and slender.'

All eyes turned to Lady Cuthbertson's fingers, which were short and stubby.

'Elaine,' said Lord Cuthbertson. But his voice was no longer pleading. It was accusing.

Lady Cuthbertson took one look at his face and

then, suddenly, bolted for the door. She threw it wide and ran out - straight into the arms of the waiting footmen.

Lord Carlton rose. 'I will take things from here,' he said.

He went out.

Lady Carlton, taking pity on Lord Cuthbertson, led him away from the rest of the stunned guests and out of the room.

There was silence for a full two minutes. And then a buzz of conversation broke out.

But that, too, soon settled down.

Then Mr Spence turned to Catherine. 'How long have you known?'

'Only since last night. As I said, it was Mrs Maltravers' sentence that made me see the light.'

'Ah, well,' sighed Mrs Maltravers complacently. 'Some of us have a gift for it.' Although what "it" was, she did not care to elucidate.

Then Lord Gilstead's voice broke into the conversation. 'I can believe that Lady Cuthbertson allowed her charge to drown so that she could become Lady Cuthbertson, but I am still not convinced that she killed Miss Winter.'

'Of course she did!' said Frederick Maltravers.

'No.' Lord Gilstead turned to Catherine. 'You see, the voice that offered Miss Winter the ring was a man's.'

'That troubled me, too,' admitted Catherine. 'Until I remembered Mr Spence's play. As I reminded you before, Miss Rivers took on the part of Sir Toby Entwhistle and played it surprisingly well.'

'Your point?'

'When Lady Cuthbertson told her to play the part, do you remember what Miss Rivers said?'

Lord Gilstead looked blank. But then his face began to show a look of understanding. 'She said, "The part would be played so much better by you."'

'At the time I took it for her usual flattery,' said Catherine. 'But later I wondered whether it could have been the truth. So when I wrote to Mr and Mrs Winter to ask them whether Miss Fanshaw had been able to swim I also asked them whether she had ever taken part in any charades.' She handed the letter to Lord Gilstead. He read it carefully and his eyebrows raised.

'Well? What does it say?' demanded old Mrs Dunstan.

'It says Miss Fanshaw was a gifted mimic. She joined in readily with dramatic entertainments if an extra person was needed, and could take on the part of a man as successfully as the part of a woman.'

'But what I don't understand is, why give Miss Winter a ring at all?' asked Mr Glover, chewing his lip.

'I think that is obvious,' said Miss Dunstan, with a quick glance at Lord Amundel. 'First of all, to put Miss Winter off her guard. And secondly, so that if anyone overheard the conversation, and if murder was ever suspected, Lord Amundel - Jason, Lord Amundel, that is - would be blamed.'

Catherine glanced at Lord Amundel. Through all of this he had sat stony faced. She longed to go to him, but she could not do so now. Would he forgive her? She had given him no inkling of her suspicions, but would he understand that she had done it for the best of reasons? That she had not wanted to accuse anyone until she was sure. And that even then she had said nothing, in case Lady Cuthbertson had somehow overheard and taken to her heels? She did not know.

'And so she killed Miss Winter to protect her guilty secret,' said Mr Spence.

'Some women will do anything for a title,' said Mrs Maltravers virtuously; a comment to which no one made any reply.

Then Melissa Maltravers piped up. 'I wondered. She said something to me. Sophie Winter. Just before she died. "I wonder why old Fanshaw says she can't swim." I didn't know what she meant. I didn't know who "old Fanshaw" was. We were arranging a swimming party down by the lake,' Melissa explained. 'We had met whilst out riding - Mama, Clarissa, Charry and I were staying nearby - and had struck up a friendship. Sophie told me she loved swimming. We were going to ask Clarissa and Felicity, and Lady Cuthbertson and some of the girls I was staying with. We knew it was no use asking Mother because she hates the water. But I see now what Sophie meant. She'd been going to ask Lady Cuthbertson to join us, but someone said Lady Cuthbertson had told her she couldn't swim. Sophie wasn't very interested at the time, but later, she wondered.'

'That's right.' It was the Reverend Mr Lucas who spoke. 'Miss Winter had asked me in a round about way whether people should lie. I said, of course, that they should not. Then she asked me, if one knew someone was lying, should one expose them?'

'And what did you say?' asked Catherine.

'I said that unless it was a matter of life or death I thought not.'

'Life or death,' mused Catherine. 'At the time Miss Winter spoke to you she would have thought it an innocent lie and decided to say nothing about it. But perhaps later she began to be unsure. She may well have heard the story of Lord Cuthbertson's half-brother and learned that the little boy had drowned. I wonder if that was what she wanted to see you about on the day she died.'

'So she wanted to see me? That is what Amundel thought, as well. Only he asked if she had already done so.'

'Her journal made it clear she wanted to talk to you,' said Catherine. 'Presumably she wanted to ask you for further advice. Because, if she had heard the story of the little boy, she might have come to realise that Lady Cuthbertson's lie *was* a matter of life and death.'

The Reverend Mr Lucas shook his head. 'Poor girl.'

As Catherine watched the genuine sadness on his face for the death of Miss Winter she shivered, realising how close she had been to condemning an innocent man, and was glad she had been determined to find proof before accusing anyone. She realised now that Lady Cuthbertson's hints at an attachment between Mr Lucas and Miss Rivers had been pure invention, designed to confuse Catherine and throw her off the true scent.

'I'm sure you suspected me,' said Mr Spence, with a lively twinkle in his eye.

Catherine was about to deny it, but laughed instead. 'Well, you did seem keen to have a play performed at Drury Lane.'

'And so I am. But not at that expense.'

'I'm surprised you didn't suspect me,' said Mr Glover morosely. 'Every young lady I fall in love with seems to meet a grisly end.'

'Nonsense!' said old Mrs Dunstan from the corner. 'Every young lady who threatens Lady Cuthbertson comes to a grisly end.'

Mr Glover suddenly brightened. 'That's true. It's Lady Cuthbertson who's the jinx, not me.'

'You fall in love again, m'boy. I've got a daughter here who'd just suit!'

Mr Glover gave an embarrassed laugh.

Lord Gilstead looked across at Miss Dunstan and suddenly smiled. 'You may not have your daughter with you for ever,' he said.

Catherine was startled. But then she looked at Lord Gilstead more closely. He was older than she had taken him for. His military carriage and lean figure disguised the fact that he was somewhere over fifty years of age. He was home from the war. Why should he not marry? Not some giddy young thing, but a sweet-tempered woman whose only defect was garrulousness. And even that, if she had plenty of company, would soon be cured.

'Well I never!' exclaimed old Mrs Dunstan, dumbfounded. 'Never see what's going on under your own nose!'

'And you, Lord Amundel,' said Mrs Maltravers nonchalantly, 'what will you do now?'

Lord Amundel roused himself. 'I will go back to London.'

'We will look forward to seeing you at the Little Season, will we not, girls?' asked Mrs Maltravers archly.

Clarissa looked embarrassed, Melissa nonchalant, and Felicity glanced at Frederick Maltravers.

'No,' said Mrs Dunstan again, with a sly look at Mrs Maltravers, 'never see what's going on under your own nose.'

Slowly, the party began to break up. Mrs Maltravers went off to discuss the whole thing, and particularly her own splendid part in it, with the Reverend Mr Lucas; the three Maltravers girls relived all the grisly horror of it with the Thomas boys; Mrs Dunstan claimed young Mr Glover and told him she had a granddaughter who was just his age; Lord Amundel left the room by himself; and Mr Spence wandered over to the window in a fit of abstraction as he planned his next play.

'Miss Morton.' Catherine heard herself addressed by Lord Gilstead as she left the room.

'Lord Gilstead?'

'May I offer you a turn around the gardens?'

'Please do.'

'It was kind of you not to mention my part in all this,' he said, as they strolled together across the lawns.

Catherine did not quite know what to say.

'I know you are aware of the fact that it was I who overheard the conversation between Miss Winter and her murderer - or perhaps I should say murderess.' Seeing her puzzled look he said, 'Amundel told me. He also told me that he learnt about it from the Reverend Mr Lucas, and warned me that if I wanted the matter kept secret I should have a word with the good Reverend.'

'I did not want to pry into your personal affairs,' said Catherine. 'But Felicity Maltravers had seen you going into Miss Simpson's room and it seemed suspicious. And . . . '

'And you had heard rumours that a young lady I was acquainted with on the Continent came to a bad end?'

Catherine nodded.

He sighed. 'Her name was Susan, and she was the daughter of my cousin. My cousin and I were very close when we were children, but then she made a bad marriage - married beneath her - and was cut off from the family.'

Married beneath her, thought Catherine. So that was what the milliner had meant by a "fallen woman"!

'But she and I still kept in touch,' went on Lord Gilstead. 'I gave her what help I could, and when she died I promised to keep an eye on her two daughters, Susan and Mary. Two years ago, when I was home on leave after Napoleon's abdication, I visited Whitegates Manor. I must confess that the proximity of the Manor to my cousin's two daughters influenced my decision to visit. I knew I would have a chance to see them.

'Could you not simply have called on them?'

He hesitated. 'No. You see, their father was so incensed at the way his wife was treated by her family —'

'By cutting her off, you mean?'

'Yes. That when he knew I was still in touch, he forbade all further contact.'

'And so you arranged to meet them in the woodland?'

'It seemed safer than meeting in the village - there

was less chance of their father hearing of it. But as things happened, I saw only Mary.'

'And whilst you were talking to her, you overheard Lady Cuthbertson speaking to Miss Winter.'

'Yes. And misunderstood what I had heard. Something for which I find it hard to forgive myself. Because of my evidence, young Amundel was suspected and finally killed himself.'

'You must not blame yourself. I know that Lord Amundel doesn't.'

'That is generous of him.'

'Besides, that is not why he killed himself. He killed himself because he hadn't kept his appointment with his love.'

They walked across the terrace and looked down at the rose gardens.

'I should not ask,' said Catherine. 'But the young lady on the Continent -?'

'Susan. Shortly before my visit two years ago she had fallen in love with a soldier, and she followed him to the Continent. Her sister, Mary, told me about her infatuation when I visited Whitegates, and I was very concerned, as you can no doubt imagine. It took me almost a year to track her down, which I finally did just before the battle of Waterloo. However, I found her too late. She had succumbed to drink, and died shortly afterwards. My only consolation is that I was able to give her some protection and comfort at the end, and that she died in my arms.'

Catherine was silent. She could quite see how this fact would have led to gossip.

'I'm sorry,' she said. The words, as always, were inadequate, but he seemed to take some comfort, if not from the words, from the feeling that lay behind them.

'And that is why I returned to Whitegates. To keep up my contact with Mary.'

They turned and walked back across the lawns.

'But why were you in Miss Simpson's room?' asked Catherine.

'I was concerned for her. She had confided in me, you see, and told me she did not believe Lord Amundel was the murderer. I, too, doubted it, and felt responsible.'

'Because it was your evidence detailing a conversation about a ring that had led to him being suspected?'

'Yes. I could not find her that morning. No one seemed to know where she had gone. I had made it my business to keep an eye on her, and at last, worried, I went to her room. She was not there. You know the rest.'

Catherine sighed. Yes, she knew.

'Will you stay here?' Lord Gilstead asked.

Catherine nodded. 'Yes. I believe I will. Lady Carlton will need my support.'

'I commend your sentiment, but you must not push yourself too hard. You have been under a considerable amount of strain.'

'Perhaps, later, I will spend a few weeks by the sea. And you?'

'It is time I settled down,' he said.

She smiled. 'I hope you will be very happy.'

His eyes twinkled. 'I will wish you the same.'

Chapter Eighteen

'Thank goodness it's all over.' Sally, hanging away Catherine's clothes, spoke from the heart.

'Yes. At last.'

'Lady Cuthbertson,' said Sally. 'I never would have guessed. Do you think she meant to do it?'

'Meant to let the boy drown?' asked Catherine. 'I don't know. She may have planned it - the boy was mischievous by all accounts, and it could be that she planted the idea of leaping from boat to boat in his mind, in the hope that he would fall in the lake - or she may just have taken advantage of the situation. But whatever the case, she planned the other three murders.'

'It was lucky you got her to say where the ring was found. You'd no other way of proving it - except to ask the gardener, and his word wouldn't have counted for much, especially against Lady Cuthbertson's.'

'I know. That was why it was so important that I made her declare it was found in the woodland. Otherwise, when I confronted her with the picture and proved the ring belonged to her, she could just have said she'd dropped it in the stables, or in the rose garden, or indeed in the drawing-room, and denied it was the ring used in Miss Winter's murder.'

'And a good thing you'd got her to tell everyone it

belonged to Miss Rivers. Otherwise she could have denied saying it and pretended she'd never tried to put you on the wrong scent.'

Catherine nodded. 'I knew I had to get her to prove both points for me: that she had tried to mislead me by saying the ring was not hers - not the act of an innocent woman - and by saying that it had been found in the woodland where Miss Winter was murdered. I pretended to believe that the Reverend Mr Lucas was the murderer, even when I had realised that it was Lady Cuthbertson, so that I could induce her to make both declarations, which she did in the belief that she was incriminating him.'

'Though you believed it was him to begin with. You believed all that faradiddle about Miss Rivers being sweet on Mr Lucas.'

'Yes. I did.'

'What I still don't see is, how did you know about the portrait?'

'Miss Rivers was talking about it one day. She said that Lady Cuthbertson had had a portrait of herself moved into the attic. I didn't think anything about it at the time, but once I suspected Lady Cuthbertson and began to ask myself if the ring could be hers, I remembered about the portrait. It occurred to me that if Lady Cuthbertson had been wearing the ring when the portrait was painted she may well have had it moved so that if the ring ever came to light it could not be traced to her.'

'So that it couldn't link her to the murder,' said Sally.

'Exactly.'

'Still, I'm surprised Lord Cuthbertson didn't

recognise the ring as soon as you took it out of your reticule.'

'I am not,' said Catherine. 'Lord Cuthbertson is short-sighted.'

'But how did you get the picture?' asked Sally, pausing in the act of laying out a silk chemise.

'I enlisted Lord Amundel's help. He sent his valet to get it. The man must be something of an actor himself, because he managed to persuade Lady Cuthbertson's housekeeper that he had come from Lady Cuthbertson.'

'And then he went to see the Winters and asked them if Miss Fanshaw could swim?'

'Yes. Their letter, brought back by Lord Amundel's valet, was very helpful. It said that Miss Fanshaw had spent some time in Cornwall after leaving her seminary and had learnt how to swim whilst there. She had then taught Miss Winter the art. They also confirmed that Miss Fanshaw was a gifted actress who often took men's parts in charades and plays.'

'Which was just the proof you needed.' Sally paused and then said nonchalantly, 'It's lucky Lord Amundel was willing to help.'

Catherine nodded. 'It is.'

'It's not every man that would send his valet off on what might turn out to be a wild goose chase just for a woman,' Sally remarked.

'No indeed.'

'And?'

'And?' asked Catherine.

'And what are you going to say?'

'Say when?'

'When he asks you to marry him.'

What indeed? wondered Catherine later that day as she wandered through the rose garden.

A part of her thought he would not propose to her on such a short acquaintance, but another part of her remembered every significant word and glance, the way he had waltzed with her, held her, kissed her. He affected her like no other man and she did not know whether she was more curious, exhilarated or afraid to find out where that would lead her.The scent of the roses drifted up to her on the breeze. It had been a good idea to come out into the garden. It gave her time to think. She did not want to see Lord Amundel until she had unravelled at least some of her feelings for him. She had seen him several times that afternoon, but always in company. She did not feel equal to seeing him alone.

But her tranquillity was short-lived. She had just reached the end of the rose gardens, and was stopping to smell a delicate yellow bloom, when she heard the sound of footsteps crunching on gravel and a minute later Lord Amundel came into view.

She straightened up when she saw him, her heart beginning to race. It was like this every time she saw him, and not only because of his looks. Undeniably his dark hair, high cheekbones, bronzed skin and brooding dark eyes attracted her, but there was a deeper connection, something she had never felt with any man before. It was as though she belonged with him.

He stopped some distance away from her, searching her face, then walked towards her.

'You have been avoiding me,' he said.

'No. I —' she broke off. Her mouth was so dry it was difficult to speak.

He was standing right in front of her. She wanted to turn her face up so that she could see him clearly, but instead she found herself looking at the ground in confusion.

'Miss Morton. Catherine. I have to return to my estate, my business here is done, but I cannot bear to leave you.' He sank to one knee. 'Will you do me the honour – the very great honour – of becoming my wife?'

Catherine's face broke into a dazzling smile. Now that the moment had come she knew exactly what to say. She had enjoyed being single, and she would happily have remained so, if she had not met him. But she had met him, and he was the one man in the world who could have persuaded her into matrimony.

'Oh, yes,' she said, taking his hands and raising him to his feet. 'I will.'

Printed in Poland
by Amazon Fulfillment
Poland Sp. z o.o., Wrocław

59389796R00128